CENTRAL   Short story Index

Rosen, Kenneth, comp.
  The man to send rain clouds; contemporary
stories by American Indians. Ed. and with
an introd. by Kenneth Rosen. Illus. by R.
C. Gorman & Aaron Yava.   Viking [c1974]
          illus.

  "A Richard Seaver book."

  1. American literature - Indian authors
  2. Indians of North America - Fiction 3.
  Short stories   I. Title
  1/74   73-6086

0115

THE MAN TO SEND RAIN CLOUDS

The Man to

CONTEMPORARY STORIES

EDITED AND WIT
AN INTRODUCTION B

A RICHARD SEAVER BOO

Send Rain Clouds

BY AMERICAN INDIANS

Kenneth Rosen

ILLUSTRATIONS BY R. C. GORMAN & AARON YAVA

THE VIKING PRESS / NEW YORK

Illustrations by R. C. Gorman on pages 14, 20, 28, 32, 39, 46, 51, 65, 85, 89, 156

Illustrations by Aaron Yava on pages 70, 76, 78, 81, 114, 130, 144, 166, 168

Two of the stories in this book are reprinted with the kind permission of the authors and the *New Mexico Quarterly*: "The Man to Send Rain Clouds" by Leslie Chapman Silko, Copyright © 1969 by Leslie Chapman, and "Kaiser and the War" by Simon J. Ortiz, Copyright © 1969 by Simon J. Ortiz.

ACKNOWLEDGMENTS

Two Ford Foundation grants, awarded to me by Dickinson College, Carlisle, Pennsylvania, helped ensure the body's survival while the soul enriched itself. I am also sincerely grateful to the faculty and staff of the English Department of the University of New Mexico for their cooperation during my visits.

This book, of course, belongs to the contributors themselves. May their words soar.

*It is in remembering that our power lies, and our future comes.
This is the Indian way.*

—ANNA LEE WALTERS

CONTENTS

INTRODUCTION   *ix*

The Man to Send Rain Clouds   *3*
   – *Leslie Silko*

The San Francisco Indians   *9*
   – *Simon J. Ortiz*

Come, My Sons   *15*
   – *Anna Lee Walters*

Whispers from a Dead World   *27*
   – *Joseph Little*

Yellow Woman   *33*
   – *Leslie Silko*

Kaiser and the War   *47*
   – *Simon J. Ortiz*

Nowhere to Go   *61*
   – *R. C. Gorman*

vii

Impressions on Turning Wombward   *66*
– *Joseph Little*

Tony's Story   *69*
– *Leslie Silko*

A Story of Ríos and Juan Jesús   *79*
– *Simon J. Ortiz*

Chapter I   *82*
– *Anna Lee Walters*

Uncle Tony's Goat   *93*
– *Leslie Silko*

The Killing of a State Cop   *101*
– *Simon J. Ortiz*

Zuma Chowt's Cave   *109*
– *Opal Lee Popkes*

A Geronimo Story   *128*
– *Leslie Silko*

The End of Old Horse   *145*
– *Simon J. Ortiz*

Bravura   *149*
– *Leslie Silko*

Saves a Leader   *155*
– *Larry Littlebird and the members of Circle Film*

from Humaweepi, the Warrior Priest   *161*
– *Leslie Silko*

NOTES BY THE CONTRIBUTORS   *169*

INTRODUCTION

When a few years ago the Kiowa Indian N. Scott Momaday was awarded the Pulitzer Prize for his novel *House Made of Dawn*, it seemed as though contemporary American Indian authors were finally going to receive the exposure and recognition that had so long eluded them. In fact, more and more Indian poets, particularly those from the southwestern part of the United States, are now beginning to see their work in print, but contemporary fiction by American Indians is still a rarity. This collection is an attempt to bring to the surface a small but important and growing body of literature that has until now been virtually ignored.

Most of the stories in this volume were written by young American Indian writers, and were culled from among the forty or so pieces of fiction I was able to discover in the course of a two-year search. If more has been written, I would hope that publication of the present work would incite the authors to seek publication in turn. I would also hope that it might encourage other Indian authors of the rising generation to set down on paper, no matter what the problems of language, their thoughts and memories and desires. It is my conviction that what is going on in the minds and hearts of American Indians today can best be told by Indians themselves, through their fiction.

One must recall that Indian storytelling is an essentially
oral tradition, and while anthropologists have for years de-
lighted us with the wise and colorful folk tales they have
transcribed from Indian informants, the works in this collection
are another matter altogether. One senses in many of the stories
the presence of tradition, but it is like a drum beating in the
background, at times distant, at times closer and more insistent.
Yet, almost without exception here, the writers are not naïve
Indians transmitting an untouched heritage to scholars, but
white-educated Indians bitterly aware of their "inferior" place in
white-controlled society and of the fact that theirs is a culture
threatened with extinction. One senses, too, that they are
struggling to bear witness to those searing facts through a
non-Indian genre, the short story.

The insistent drums of tradition are very much in evidence
in some of the works, such as those of Anna Lee Walters, who in
one of her pieces provides a touchingly dignified transposition
into English of a sage grandfather's advice to the young of his
tribe to listen to the drums in their hearts given to their people
by Great Buffalo. The drums are muted, or virtually silent, in
sketches such as Simon Ortiz's describing Indians' confrontation
with white culture today: a "crazy" reservation brave who goes
to prison rather than join the white man's army; an old chief
looking for his granddaughter, who has gone to San Francisco to
become a secretary; an Indian ex-marine who kills a state cop.
The same is true of R. C. Gorman's story of a Navajo hitchhiker
telling the white sailor who has picked him up about the old
days when Apaches and Navajos had *fun* fighting each other.
When the sailor asks the Indian where he wants to get out, the
answer is "Anywhere," because, symbolically, the Indian knows
he is going nowhere.

A separate word must be said about the work of Leslie
Silko, a Laguna Pueblo Indian whose stories are already so
spare, so rich, so finely honed as to stand as genuine literary
works of unquestioned value. Using Indian lore and history as a

kind of counterpoint to her special music, she writes with a
depth and intensity which, to my mind, set her work apart and
mark her as a talent from whom we can expect new, important
work. In the title story, "The Man to Send Rain Clouds," she
offers a beautifully understated celebration of the death of a
beloved Indian grandfather. In "Yellow Woman," she tells of an
Indian woman who tries to convince herself, and half succeeds,
that the cattle rustler she has met and slept with may be one of
the ka'tsina spirits that have haunted women's imaginations in
her tribe from time immemorial. "Tony's Story" tells, again, of
an ex-serviceman killing a harassing cop. In Leslie Silko's hands,
the theme becomes a potent symbol of the age-old conflict
between the invading whites and the Indians they relentlessly
pursue. It is interesting, and perhaps noteworthy, that two
stories in this volume, by two different authors, deal with this
same theme of violence and death of the white intruder.

No matter who the author, these stories are all marked with
an extremely poignant, elegiac tone and a deeply felt sadness.
All these writers are acutely aware that their once-great culture
is being ruthlessly stamped out by a morally inferior white
culture, and all of them manage, despite a certain clumsiness at
times with a language not their own, to give the reader some
sense of what it is like to live in a cultural twilight, in the margin
of a society to which they do not belong, to which they cannot
relate, and about which they feel only pity or scorn.

How did this collection come into being? In 1969, while I
was a graduate student at the University of New Mexico, I read
an unpublished short story by an Indian classmate. "I will be
walking in the middle of your soul," a line from a love
incantation of the Oklahoma Cherokees, fairly describes my
initial reaction to the story. The author had combined remem-
brance of things past with present-day realities and future
aspirations to create an organic work that was wholly accessible
to the reader. I felt as if I had entered a very private world in

which there was no distinction between subjective and objective entities.

Subsequent investigation showed that very few contemporary short stories by American Indians had ever been published. But that did not necessarily mean that stories were not being written. Questioning other young Indians, I began to suspect that there might be a small but significant body of contemporary fiction being produced by writers who obviously had few outlets for their work, and who most certainly had scant knowledge of each other's existence as writers.

In 1970 I decided to try to track down any Indians who were writing fiction and, if I found a sufficient number, gather their work into a volume. Failing this, I would try to find outlets for individual stories of merit. I concentrated on Indians of the Southwest for the same reason that John R. Milton did when he edited *The American Indian Speaks*. The various Indian cultures are stronger, and the arts flourish to a greater extent, in the Southwest simply because the cultures are older and more firmly established there, and because the climate, both palpable and impalpable, seems to be more conducive to artistic expression. In the best Hopi tradition of always being prepared, "I studied clouds and paid close attention to my dreams in order to escape being trapped by storms too far from shelter" as I began my quest.

The Bureau of Indian Affairs office in Albuquerque was one of my first stops. The people there were friendly and interested in my project, but they had no information about individual Indians who might be writing fiction. They offered me a list of Pueblo and Apache people who were working on traditional tales, legends, and songs; and it was suggested that I contact the Pueblo Council and the Institute of American Indian Art in Santa Fe for possible leads. I visited the Pueblo Council and met most of the governors of the various pueblos, but I soon realized that a search on an individual basis would be my only hope of finding any manuscripts at all. Leslie Silko, a young lady from

Laguna Pueblo who is both a poet and a writer of fiction, and who is currently teaching at the Navajo Community College at Many Farms, Arizona, offered me the first stories I received for this collection. She also gave me the names of several Indian friends who might be doing some writing of their own. The pattern of my search was thus established: word-of-mouth, door-to-door, town-to-town, with no logical sequence to my travels except the suggestion from some Indian or Anglo, "I hear so-and-so is writing stories or tales."

I spent some time in all the pueblos and read stories written by people from Acoma, Laguna, Isleta, Santo Domingo, Santa Clara, San Juan, San Ildefonso, Taos, Tesuque, Cochiti, and Zuni. Leslie Silko, Simon Ortiz, and Larry Littlebird are contributors to this collection who are of Pueblo ancestry. Mr. Ortiz, who has a new book of poetry scheduled for publication this year, is from Acoma Pueblo and now lives in Albuquerque. Mr. Littlebird, who lives in Sante Fe, is a very active young man. In addition to being the director of an all-Indian film company (Circle Film), he is also a painter and graphic artist and the star of the still-to-be-released film version of *House Made of Dawn.*

R. C. Gorman, a Navajo who grew up on the reservation at Chinle, Arizona, is a painter who has a gallery in Taos, New Mexico. Mr. Gorman's paintings hang in several of the major art museums of this country; his story in this collection is his first published piece of fiction.

From Taos I went north and west to the Ute Mountain and Jicarilla Apache reservations, armed with the names of two young Indian writers. The bureaucracy which, as I often found during my search, so effectively surrounds the American Indian proved most effective in the northernmost part of New Mexico: there are young Indians writing fiction in that part of the country, but I was unable to uncover any stories from them for inclusion here.

Joseph Little is a Mescalero Apache from the southern part of New Mexico. His name was given to me by a Jicarilla Apache hitchhiker I picked up as I was returning from my unsuccessful trip to the Ute Mountain area. I located Mr. Little in Albuquerque, where he was a student at the university, and he offered me two stories he had recently completed. Another student at the university suggested I contact Mrs. Anna Lee Walters, a Pawnee/Otoe, but nobody seemed to know where she lived. With the help of the people at the Institute of American Indian Art, I was finally able to get in touch with her by phone. She was happy to have her work read and agreed to send some stories to me. Opal Lee Popkes is of Choctaw descent. "Zuma Chowt's Cave" is an extract from her first novel, *Forgotten Woman.* Born in Texas, she now makes her home in Missouri. Aaron Yava, a Navajo/Pueblo living at Many Farms, has kindly contributed some original art to the book.

In the course of almost two years I was able to locate and read, as I have mentioned, some forty contemporary short stories written by American Indians. It is my belief that these are only a small sample of what is currently being produced, but the task of searching out new material is a difficult and often frustrating one. Poetry and traditional tales still seem to be the dominent genres for American Indian writers, but fiction is attracting the efforts of more and more young people who have left the pueblos and the reservations and who are faced with the monumental task of somehow reconciling an inherent concept of tradition with a contemporary non-Indian world in which the exploitation of the individual talent is forever being encouraged. Young Indian writers, each in his or her own way, seem to be trying to deal with those dichotomies so central to the non-Indian world—natural/unnatural, objective/subjective, good/evil, functional/artistic—without losing sight of the traditionally organic view of existence which is, after all, the essential legacy each of these writers has inherited.

K.R.

THE MAN TO SEND RAIN CLOUDS

−Leslie Silko

The Man to Send Rain Clouds

ONE

They found him under a big cottonwood tree. His Levi jacket and pants were faded light-blue so that he had been easy to find. The big cottonwood tree stood apart from a small grove of winterbare cottonwoods which grew in the wide, sandy arroyo. He had been dead for a day or more, and the sheep had wandered and scattered up and down the arroyo. Leon and his brother-in-law, Ken, gathered the sheep and left them in the pen at the sheep camp before they returned to the cottonwood tree. Leon waited under the tree while Ken drove the truck through the deep sand to the edge of the arroyo. He squinted up at the sun and unzipped his jacket—it sure was hot for this time of year. But high and northwest the blue mountains were still deep in snow. Ken came sliding down the low, crumbling bank about fifty yards down, and he was bringing the red blanket.

Before they wrapped the old man, Leon took a piece of string out of his pocket and tied a small gray feather in the old man's long white hair. Ken gave him the paint. Across the brown wrinkled forehead he drew a streak of white and along the high cheekbones he drew a strip of blue paint. He paused and watched Ken throw pinches of corn meal and pollen into the

wind that fluttered the small gray feather. Then Leon painted
with yellow under the old man's broad nose, and finally, when
he had painted green across the chin, he smiled.

"Send us rain clouds, Grandfather." They laid the bundle in
the back of the pickup and covered it with a heavy tarp before
they started back to the pueblo.

They turned off the highway onto the sandy pueblo road.
Not long after they passed the store and post office they saw
Father Paul's car coming toward them. When he recognized
their faces he slowed his car and waved for them to stop. The
young priest rolled down the car window.

"Did you find old Teofilo?" he asked loudly.

Leon stopped the truck. "Good morning, Father. We were
just out to the sheep camp. Everything is O.K. now."

"Thank God for that. Teofilo is a very old man. You really
shouldn't allow him to stay at the sheep camp alone."

"No, he won't do that any more now."

"Well, I'm glad you understand. I hope I'll be seeing you at
Mass this week—we missed you last Sunday. See if you can get
old Teofilo to come with you." The priest smiled and waved at
them as they drove away.

TWO

Louise and Teresa were waiting. The table was set for
lunch, and the coffee was boiling on the black iron stove. Leon
looked at Louise and then at Teresa.

"We found him under a cottonwood tree in the big arroyo
near sheep camp. I guess he sat down to rest in the shade and
never got up again." Leon walked toward the old man's bed.
The red plaid shawl had been shaken and spread carefully over
the bed, and a new brown flannel shirt and pair of stiff new
Levis were arranged neatly beside the pillow. Louise held the
screen door open while Leon and Ken carried in the red blanket.

He looked small and shriveled, and after they dressed him in the new shirt and pants he seemed more shrunken.

It was noontime now because the church bells rang the Angelus. They ate the beans with hot bread, and nobody said anything until after Teresa poured the coffee.

Ken stood up and put on his jacket. "I'll see about the gravediggers. Only the top layer of soil is frozen. I think it can be ready before dark."

Leon nodded his head and finished his coffee. After Ken had been gone for a while, the neighbors and clanspeople came quietly to embrace Teofilo's family and to leave food on the table because the gravediggers would come to eat when they were finished.

THREE

The sky in the west was full of pale-yellow light. Louise stood outside with her hands in the pockets of Leon's green army jacket that was too big for her. The funeral was over, and the old men had taken their candles and medicine bags and were gone. She waited until the body was laid into the pickup before she said anything to Leon. She touched his arm, and he noticed that her hands were still dusty from the corn meal that she had sprinkled around the old man. When she spoke, Leon could not hear her.

"What did you say? I didn't hear you."

"I said that I had been thinking about something."

"About what?"

"About the priest sprinkling holy water for Grandpa. So he won't be thirsty."

Leon stared at the new moccasins that Teofilo had made for the ceremonial dances in the summer. They were nearly hidden by the red blanket. It was getting colder, and the wind pushed gray dust down the narrow pueblo road. The sun was approaching the long mesa where it disappeared during the winter. Louise stood there shivering and watching his face. Then he zipped up his jacket and opened the truck door. "I'll see if he's there."

FOUR

Ken stopped the pickup at the church, and Leon got out; and then Ken drove down the hill to the graveyard where people were waiting. Leon knocked at the old carved door with its symbols of the Lamb. While he waited he looked up at the twin bells from the king of Spain with the last sunlight pouring around them in their tower.

The priest opened the door and smiled when he saw who it was. "Come in! What brings you here this evening?"

The priest walked toward the kitchen, and Leon stood with his cap in his hand, playing with the earflaps and examining the living room—the brown sofa, the green armchair, and the brass lamp that hung down from the ceiling by links of chain. The priest dragged a chair out of the kitchen and offered it to Leon.

"No thank you, Father. I only came to ask you if you would bring your holy water to the graveyard."

The priest turned away from Leon and looked out the window at the patio full of shadows and the dining-room windows of the nuns' cloister across the patio. The curtains were heavy, and the light from within faintly penetrated; it was impossible to see the nuns inside eating supper. "Why didn't you tell me he was dead? I could have brought the Last Rites anyway."

Leon smiled. "It wasn't necessary, Father."

The priest stared down at his scuffed brown loafers and the worn hem of his cassock. "For a Christian burial it was necessary."

His voice was distant, and Leon thought that his blue eyes looked tired.

"It's O.K. Father, we just want him to have plenty of water."

The priest sank down into the green chair and picked up a glossy missionary magazine. He turned the colored pages full of lepers and pagans without looking at them.

"You know I can't do that, Leon. There should have been the Last Rites and a funeral Mass at the very least."

Leon put on his green cap and pulled the flaps down over his ears. "It's getting late, Father. I've got to go."

When Leon opened the door Father Paul stood up and said, "Wait." He left the room and came back wearing a long brown overcoat. He followed Leon out the door and across the dim churchyard to the adobe steps in front of the church. They both stooped to fit through the low adobe entrance. And when they started down the hill to the graveyard only half of the sun was visible above the mesa.

The priest approached the grave slowly, wondering how they had managed to dig into the frozen ground; and then he remembered that this was New Mexico, and saw the pile of cold loose sand beside the hole. The people stood close to each other with little clouds of steam puffing from their faces. The priest looked at them and saw a pile of jackets, gloves, and scarves in the yellow, dry tumbleweeds that grew in the graveyard. He looked at the red blanket, not sure that Teofilo was so small, wondering if it wasn't some perverse Indian trick—something they did in March to ensure a good harvest—wondering if maybe old Teofilo was actually at sheep camp corraling the sheep for the night. But there he was, facing into a cold dry wind and squinting at the last sunlight, ready to bury a red wool blanket while the faces of his parishioners were in shadow with the last warmth of the sun on their backs.

His fingers were stiff, and it took him a long time to twist the lid off the holy water. Drops of water fell on the red blanket and soaked into dark icy spots. He sprinkled the grave and the water disappeared almost before it touched the dim, cold sand; it reminded him of something—he tried to remember what it was, because he thought if he could remember he might understand this. He sprinkled more water; he shook the container until it was empty, and the water fell through the light from sundown like August rain that fell while the sun was still shining, almost evaporating before it touched the wilted squash flowers.

The wind pulled at the priest's brown Franciscan robe and swirled away the corn meal and pollen that had been sprinkled on the blanket. They lowered the bundle into the ground, and they didn't bother to untie the stiff pieces of new rope that were tied around the ends of the blanket. The sun was gone, and over on the highway the eastbound lane was full of headlights. The priest walked away slowly. Leon watched him climb the hill, and when he had disappeared within the tall, thick walls, Leon turned to look up at the high blue mountains in the deep snow that reflected a faint red light from the west. He felt good because it was finished, and he was happy about the sprinkling of the holy water; now the old man could send them big thunderclouds for sure.

—Simon J. Ortiz

The
San Francisco
Indians

The Chief and a couple of members of his tribe went to the American Indian Center at Mission and 16th. They had walked all the way from their street. A lock hung on the door of the Center, and they stood by the door wondering whether they should go back, call somebody up, or wait around.

"I wonder where they're all at," one of them said.

"Maybe it's a day off or something," another offered.

The Chief pushed against the door again and searched for a notice or something. He read the Fuck FBIs scribble again and felt sad. "I guess there isn't going to be anybody here," he said and pulled his blanket tighter to ward off the cold. He motioned to the others and they began to leave. "We'll come back later," the Chief said.

At that moment a man walked around the corner and looked up at the plastic sign reading American Indian Center.

One of the Chief's companions called, "Hey, Chief Black Bear." The Chief and the others stopped and watched the man.

The man was around seventy years old. His gray suit was wrinkled and his shoes were scuffed. He looked at the door with the lock and then stepped back into the street. He held a grip bag in his hand.

"Hey, there's an Indian," one of the tribal members said. He smiled happily.

"Yes, there's an Indian," Chief Black Bear said. He straightened up and walked toward the Indian. The Indian man watched them approach.

"Hello," the Chief said. He offered a handshake.

"Hello," the Indian said, shaking hands lightly. He was nervous, and he looked at the pavement and then at the young man with the blanket and beads before him. The others, both young men also, stood to one side. They were not as dressed in Indian attire as their chief was.

The Chief and his companions noticed that the Indian was very tired. They felt his tiredness and his age. The Chief said, "We want to invite you to our home. It is not far from here."

"Yes," the Indian said. "But first, I have to find out where all the Indians go. Is this where all the Indians go?" He indicated the locked-up Center.

"Yes," Chief Black Bear said. "They come here, but not all of them. They're all over the city. Some are up on the street."

"Yes, Indians are everywhere," the Indian said.

"Come with us, and you can come back later when you have eaten and rested."

The Indian thought about this for a while. He didn't know where to go. He had come this far, and he didn't know where to go.

"I came to look for my grandchild. She came to go to school in Oakland, to learn about business work, months ago. She wrote to tell us she was O.K. But we got letters from the school that she was not going any more, and then she stopped writing. I asked the government, but they don't know about her any more. I came to see her, to find her, but I haven't found her.

Someone said she came to San Francisco. That's why I came to where the Indians come. Maybe somebody knows her and where she lives."

The Chief and his tribe were saddened by the old man's search. They wanted to comfort him somehow. "There are Indians on our street," the youthful chief said. "Maybe they will know."

The Indian and Chief Black Bear and his tribe walked through gray streets busy with traffic. Some people stared at them, and some didn't. They walked up and down hills. The walking reminded the Indian of the hills and mesas at home. He couldn't see much except buildings and traffic and Chinamen hurrying to some place. Once in a while he could see the ocean to the west. He wanted to ask questions of the young men, but they were intent in their walking and were quiet.

Haight Street was crowded as usual. The Indian saw that some people were just sitting, some were walking around or driving past. He wondered if it was Sunday or a day off. There were a few dressed like the young men he walked with. Chief Black Bear and his companions called greetings to people they met. They walked into a building and up some stairs and entered a room.

"You are welcome here," Chief Black Bear said. He pointed to a small cot. "You can sit down there and sleep there, too." The other two left the room.

The Indian sat down, and he wondered if he would find his grandchild here. There was fast music coming from somewhere behind the walls, and muffled sounds came from the street. The Chief offered him a boloney sandwich and a bottle of wine.

"I'll see if I can find some Indian kids," Chief Black Bear said, and left.

After he had finished eating, the Indian lay down and closed his eyes. He was very tired. He had almost fallen asleep

when a girl's voice called, "Chief." He came fully awake to face
a girl with blond hair, wearing a colored band around her head.

"Hi," she said. "I'm looking for Chief Black Bear. I heard
he brought an Indian back." She was smiling.

"Hello," the Indian said and sat up.

They watched each other. "We have some peyote from
Mexico," the girl said. She brought a large coffee can filled with
some of the dried buttons. "We have some songs," she said and
showed him some records of Indian chants. "This will be the
first time, and we wanted someone who knows how to show us."
The girl fingered her beads.

The Indian had never seen peyote before, but he had heard
songs and prayers for the ceremonials. Maybe it will do O.K., he
thought, but he was doubtful. He didn't know the labels on the
records, but he thought the chants were not what they would
need.

"We want it to be good," the girl said. She felt some of the
old man's tiredness too, and his searching and sadness, even
without his telling her. She reached out and touched him.

The Chief came back. "There are no Indians around," he
said.

The Indian thought, Maybe they have all left for their
homes. He looked about the room and wondered if he should
leave too. Yes, maybe he should, he thought. But he had come
this far, to some place, he was tired, he had seen glimpses of the
ocean he had heard about, he had not found his grandchild, and
he did not really know where else to look. He had come to look
for her because the girl's parents had not. They said, She'll be all
right, she's grown up, our people are going some place every
day, there are Indians all over the place, she'll be O.K. And
that's why he had come.

The People were going all over the world. Indians were
everywhere. He had met some at bus stations in Arizona and

California. They stood around looking into jukeboxes, maga-
zines in their hands, and getting on and off the buses. And he
had met these San Francisco Indians. He looked over at the
Chief and the girl who sat on the floor opposite him. They
smiled at him.

"I think I'll go now," he said. And he got up to get his bag.
"Thank you for your food and wine."

"Wait," Chief Black Bear said. The girl looked worried.
And they both looked as if they would grab and hold the Indian.
"Won't you stay tonight? We want you to be with us. We have
all the things ready," the Chief said.

The Indian looked at the coffee can. "I don't know anything about the peyote stuff. I have heard the songs and prayers,
but I think you need more than that. I think I will go," he said.

"But your granddaughter, aren't you going to wait and see
if you can find somebody who knows where she is?" Chief Black
Bear asked.

"I came to look for my grandchild, but I haven't been able
to find her. I am getting to be an old man, and I am tired, and I
should be home. My grandchild will be all right, I think. Indians
are everywhere."

The Chief and the girl watched helplessly as the Indian left.
When he got down to the street, he called a cab from a bar. The
cab drove him to the bus station.

As the bus went south toward Palo Alto, the day was
getting dark. He thought of a scene a long time back. My
prayers were for rain. Pray for rain, my mother said. The *koshare*
were going to the east. They were going home. Let us go home,
brothers, they sang. I watched them with my prayers.

– *Anna Lee Walters*

Come, My Sons

Come, my sons. Sit by my side and warm my hands with yours. For I fill with pride when one of you is near. Your presence is reassuring.

I have many things to say to each of you. Lately, I have been preoccupied with thoughts that sneak into my mind. It is for this reason that I have called you by name, interrupting your play, insisting that you come to me.

My sons, you are my greatest offering to a people where many are weary from misused and unused lives. All that you are, all that you will be, it is I who have cleared the path.

You are yet boys. Soon you will be men.
And I must set you free. You are my sons,
but I do not know you. I can dream great
dreams for you, but my dreams are not
your dreams. Your life is not my life.
Yours' may end today in ways I have not
dared to think. I know this.

My sons, because my voice is clear and
steady, do not think I feel nothing.
Because my eyes are free from tears, do
not think my heart is. Just to know there
is little I can do when it comes to each of
your destinies, that terrible things could
come about, it makes me ache inside.

I wish I could be with each of you forever.
But my sons, all I can do is cry with you
or even for you when you feel pain. And
though this may be a cruel thing for me to
say and difficult for you to hear, it is true
that while I would give my life, would die
for you, my sons, I can never live for you.

Come now, we will change this talk. It
will end my foolish thoughts and we will
never speak of them again. For the lodge
that will be yours is now complete. I

cannot change it or move it. I can only
hope that it will serve you well.

Time has come to speak of things long
past. Of countless days filled with endless
nights. Of time that moved in beauty and
with ease. My sons, these things must be
heard in meaningful silence. So make
your mind wide and clean like the eastern
sky at sunrise. Wash your heart earnestly
in the tears of the "old ones" that you
may be worthy of what I will tell. For it is
said their tears have great value. They
were red and fell gently like blood. My
sons, everyone now has tears of water.

My sons, this is a story that is like a song.
A sacred song that can be sung only once.
Should we abuse it by changing it in
telling and retelling, our story would
become worthless and have little
meaning. That is the way too many
important ideas have been destroyed.

One thought passed around like dry
leaves, scattering wildly on windy days,
with no planning as to where they will
finally rest. The leaves pile up in untied
bundles. People take notice for a short
while. The leaves of red, yellow, and

orange continue to cover our mother
earth like a warm blanket. And only a few
rare people understand or care. My sons,
do you know that many burn those dying
leaves?

That is why we must use some judgment
in deciding about people and what they
should hear. Take time to find those who
deserve to listen. Take time to know those
who want to listen.

And though you shall hear this just once,
at a time when your minds are young and
uncluttered with memories that
accompany time, it will be with you
always. You will forget it only in brief
moments when all the world is yours and
you feel that there is nothing you cannot
overcome. But something or someone will
shake you and remind you of this story.
Out of the forgotten days of youth, it will
crawl like a beautiful baby you cannot
ignore. Yes, my sons, it will haunt you all
your lives and echo in your minds and
re-echo in the days when life is precious
and draws to its end.

I shall tell it now with love for each of you
and with respect for those who were

before me. It would not be sacred if I told
it otherwise. For this is truly their song.
They sang it many times, in many ways
an eternity ago.

Listen my sons! Listen to a song for life.
The words are good. The song is old.
Hear me now! Inside each of you, there
beats a drum. Drums that are never silent.
They speak and talk of life. When your
strong brown hands reach out, the drums
swell and move with pride. When your
dark laughing eyes are still and bright
with thought, the drums are whispering of
your promise as men.

I wish that your grandmothers could see
you now. I wish they could reach out and
touch you. For they were the ones who
gave their drums to you.

In the peaceful dark of yesterday they
lived strong and proud, wise and beautiful
because of their drums. Life was long and
well-lived. It died with dignity. The drums
were the reason. They made life worth
living.

If you should ask me from where the

drums came, I have no answer. I know
only that they have been for all time.
There are stories that exist even today.
The stories say that the drums lived with
the buffalo at one time. I do not know. I
am sure there are none today who really
know except the drums. You realize, my
sons, there are old, dusty, almost
forgotten songs that call the buffalo by
name. He is called with great respect, the
most honored name. He is called
"Grandfather."

Before the Grandfathers ruled is a space
in time we never speak of. We know
nothing of it. We should not flatter or
shame ourselves by pretending to know
what we do not. Yes my sons, life was
pleasant and rewarding in the days of our
grandmothers. Then all too soon Old Age
came to stay. They knew without anyone
telling them they must make room for you
and me. Now Old Age demanded more
and more of their attention. Soon he
would make them forget their drums
entirely. The handsome drums born to
make music must inevitably become
silent.

You see, my sons, this is what comes of
Old Age. By many he is greeted

graciously and accepted lovingly. In
return he is comforting and protecting,
promising nothing yet offering everything.
Unhappily by many more, he is rejected
in every possible way. They who are
guilty of this do to themselves a great
injustice, for Old Age can never truly be
rejected. And he will make that one look
foolish who appears to dismiss him. It is
then that he pulls himself to his full
height, and towering over one, he
commands respect. It is to be those that
he arrives much sooner than they expect,
claiming all the senses and robbing all of
life.

Tomorrow when he comes, you should
say that you are not prepared. You may
ask him to be generous with time. Say
that you desperately need to make him a
place where he will be proud and one that
will do him great honor. You must say
these things to him, my sons. He is
understanding and patient with only
those who are understanding and patient
with him.

Now remember, my sons, once he moves
in, it is in poor taste to ask him to move
out. He would not, you know, and there is
no way to make him. Old Age, proud and

haughty warrior that he is, has a secret as
most of us do. He admires and envies life.
There is nothing greater than his respect
for one who cherishes life. My sons, he,
never having life, yearns and rewards it.
This would be an honorable thing, to
have Old Age move aside and wait on
you.

Perhaps of all the virtues of old age, the
best known is wisdom. Only the very wise
could foresee the future of the drums. Old
Age looks well dressed in mercy. He took
pity on the drums and cared for them.

The grandmothers discussed their fate,
calling regularly on him for answers. Soon
it was decided that the drums should be
given away, but not just to anyone. No,
they must be given to a special people.

The old ones knew that someone,
someday, would need the power of the
drums. So after solemn prayers for
guidance, they decided to whom the
drums should be given. A few were given
away immediately, for there are always
those who are in need of such strength.
Many more were saved for others who
would follow in the footprints of time.

For those to come in the future, the
drums were hidden in the shelter of the
buffalo robe, because this is where the
drums lived in the beginning. The
grandmothers, though weakened by
years, remembered this and humbly
returned them.

My sons, it is important to remember. It is
in remembering that our power lies and
our future comes. This is the Indian way.

Little ones, the sun has daily searched the
skies. The moon has followed, cautiously
seeking places the sun, in anxiety, might
have overlooked. Continually the earth
was scoured by the piercing eyes of empty
years. Then finally, one morning when
night lifted her arms and tiptoed away,
one by one, you came. The sun, realizing
who you were, has since slowed his rapid
pace and watches you expectantly. The
moon has polished the silver shield she
carries to guide your moccasined feet in
the direction you choose to follow. She
has rubbed clean the faces of her children,
the stars, that one of you might take
notice of them.

My sons, I, along with the family whose
home is heaven, have waited for you. And

now, too, the grandmothers will rest
peacefully, knowing you and others like
you have finally arrived.

You understand, my sons, the
grandmothers have been patient. Time
did not control, and if time does not
control, time cannot defeat.

They have borrowed these drums from
the living soul of yesterday. They have
been examined for quality of tone. Their
voices are beautiful. Their melody is
lasting. The grandmothers have placed
them in your care. They have chosen the
warmest place that they might sing their
best. My sons, they rest upon your hearts.

Now for a short time the drums are yours.
Beat them loudly and clumsily with your
youth. For youth has always given them
reason to dance in pure delight.

Beat them tenderly and possessively with
the cautious flings of middle age. For
there are long years between childhood
and manhood. Years where questions will
rise like smoke curling from the ground

around you, clouding your vision and
threatening to bring tears.

Most of the questions will be answered by
careful reasoning. Your tongue will shout
the answer. But you will find, my sons,
that the most important questions in life
cannot be asked. The answer to those
dwells in the heart. And as most of our
people know, the heart has no tongue.

So my sons, when your steps take longer
yet become shorter, when your back
becomes bowed from the years you carry,
and when the short dark hair that now
hugs your head becomes tired gray
threads that hang in strands down your
back, you must use the drums even then.

With all your energy for their final song,
beat the drums lovingly, extracting only
the finest notes with all the skill of learned
musicians.

–Joseph Little

Whispers
from a Dead World

Aquinas, as a philosopher of being, says a creature exercises its most basic act by simply being, but in existing it tends to perfect its being.

The sun was already well on its daily ramble when Walter stepped out of the house, the ripped screen door slamming behind him. He adjusted his black cowboy hat as he walked across the dirt road that took up where his short front yard left off. He ducked through the large hole in a barbed-wire fence where the strands had been stretched apart, and threaded his way down the side of the hill toward the main highway.

Augustine's ethics are based on love and the use of the will. His ethical outlook establishes a search for earthly well-being leading to a preparation of the soul for eternal salvation. It is theocentric eudaimonism.

It wasn't quite noon when Walter stepped into the dimly lit recesses of the tribal bar. Little spots danced in front of his eyes, miniature copies of the sun that glared outside. His eyes quickly

27

adjusted, and he could make out three figures sitting on bar stools by the time he reached the counter. The bartender stood behind the counter wiping a glass, the glass resting on his stomach which his T-shirt strained to contain. Walter blinked and asked him, "Have you seen my wife?"

"Not since you two were in here together, and that was two days ago."

"Oh, well give me a Coors, will ya."

Walter was about halfway through his second drink when he felt a hand clutch his shoulder. He turned and was hit by a wave of wine-sweet breath. He looked into a pair of bloodshot eyes.

"How about a drink?"

"I'm broke."

"Don't give me that shit. How about a drink?"

"I'm broke, I told you. Go find someone else to bother."

The hand left his shoulder, and the sickly sweet wine odor dissipated, smothering a string of garbled curses.

The promptings of an informed reason and moral conscience represent an inherent tendency in the nature of man, and conformity to this nature fulfills both the cosmic plan of the creator and the direct commands of God as revealed by Scripture.

The sun was resting on the mountains when Walter finally stumbled out of the bar. Arm in arm he and a friend weaved their way down a dirt path edged by a wall of weeds. They reached the creek and flopped down on its grassy bank. They both dropped their heads into the icy water and came up shaking them. They pulled their shirt tails out of their pants and wiped their faces almost dry. On their knees, with streams of water dribbling down their chests, they burst out laughing. Slowly subsiding into fits of choking, they dragged themselves to some nearby trees, and sat leaning against the cottonwood trunks. It was almost dark now, and the crickets could be heard all around. A cool breeze swept through the limbs of the creaking cottonwoods, and the sweet smell of grass filled their nostrils.

"Hey, Paul, I thought you were working."

"I got laid off last week. Laid a bunch of us off."

"Hand me that bottle of wine."

"Hey, saw your wife last night. She was over at your brother's house."

> *. . . it is not sufficient for our conscience to be aware of the law; our will must be rectified so that it will yield to it and put it into practice. This rectification of the will is brought about by the illuminating action of the divine virtues.*

The dogs were barking wildly when Walter staggered the last few steps to the porch and wrapped his arms around one of its pole supports. He closed his eyes and his head became a black, swirling abyss. He opened them quickly and tried to focus them on the front door. He remained staring at it for a couple of minutes before he pulled himself together and attacked it. Leaning on it for support, he banged on the door with both fists and tried to curse as best his thick tongue would allow.

The door finally opened, and his brother stood facing him, hair rumpled, his face distorted by sleep, and clad only in his underwear. Walter stood rocking back and forth, trying to enunciate, "Where is my wife?" Finally he fell against his brother, making a clumsy attempt to grasp his throat. Then his head snapped back as a fist slammed into his mouth. He sailed backward off the porch and rolled to a stop in a clump of bushes. As he got to his hands and knees, he could make out the outlines of his wife's face bobbing over his brother's shoulder, and caught her curses. Then the door slammed.

. . . the nature of man is determined by the eternal law, one is in accord with the eternal law by doing what is in accord with nature. When one acts contrary to nature, one is in the wrong.

Walter had washed himself clean in the creek in the early purple light of dawn. The early morning wind whipped his hair and stirred the branches of the piñon trees into life. He had just started to trace one of the many deer trails that zigzagged along the side of the mountain slope, when he stopped and looked back down into the valley below him. Thousands of clustered sunflowers were raising their heads toward the sun as it grew over the mountain rim. Farther down, the sheen of the sinuous creek disappeared into a forest of willows. Above him the slope of the mountain swept steeply upward. Yucca plants and mesquite bushes clung tenaciously to its side, their roots lost in rocks. Way above, the demarcation of the timber line stretched like a hairline along the top of the mountain. Walter's ears caught the sound of the bluejays and robins as he started his ascent.

Man's greatest virtue is "authenticity," a kind of honesty and courage to see the world in its absurdity and to face the necessity of decisions, the recognition of their moral aspects, and the acceptance of responsibility for it.

Walter stood on a high ledge and looked down into the valley. The pines whispered about him, and his mind rode on the waves of those whispers. The sun caressed his back. And, now stripped to the waist, his body soaked in the warmth. From below, an eagle rose upward in ever-increasing circles. It stretched out its wings and rose toward the sun. Walter stretched out his arms and gave his body to the wind. And for an instant he, too, soared free. And then he traced the upward path of the eagle.

Yellow Woman

ONE

My thigh clung to his with dampness, and I watched the sun rising up through the tamaracks and willows. The small brown water birds came to the river and hopped across the mud, leaving brown scratches in the alkali-white crust. They bathed in the river silently. I could hear the water, almost at our feet where the narrow fast channel bubbled and washed green ragged moss and fern leaves. I looked at him beside me, rolled in the red blanket on the white river sand. I cleaned the sand out of the cracks between my toes, squinting because the sun was above the willow trees. I looked at him for the last time, sleeping on the white river sand.

I felt hungry and followed the river south the way we had come the afternoon before, following our footprints that were already blurred by lizard tracks and bug trails. The horses were still lying down, and the black one whinnied when he saw me but he did not get up—maybe it was because the corral was made out of thick cedar branches and the horses had not yet felt the sun like I had. I tried to look beyond the pale red mesas to the pueblo. I knew it was there, even if I could not see it, on the sandrock hill above the river, the same river that moved past me now and had reflected the moon last night.

The horse felt warm underneath me. He shook his head and pawed the sand. The bay whinnied and leaned against the gate trying to follow, and I remembered him asleep in the red blanket beside the river. I slid off the horse and tied him close to the other horse. I walked north with the river again, and the white sand broke loose in footprints over footprints.

"Wake up."

He moved in the blanket and turned his face to me with his eyes still closed. I knelt down to touch him.

"I'm leaving."

He smiled now, eyes still closed. "You are coming with me, remember?" He sat up now with his bare dark chest and belly in the sun.

"Where?"

"To my place."

"And will I come back?"

He pulled his pants on. I walked away from him, feeling him behind me and smelling the willows.

"Yellow Woman," he said.

I turned to face him. "Who are you?" I asked.

He laughed and knelt on the low, sandy bank, washing his face in the river. "Last night you guessed my name, and you knew why I had come."

I stared past him at the shallow moving water and tried to remember the night, but I could only see the moon in the water and remember his warmth around me.

"But I only said that you were him and that I was Yellow Woman—I'm not really her—I have my own name and I come from the pueblo on the other side of the mesa. Your name is Silva and you are a stranger I met by the river yesterday afternoon."

He laughed softly. "What happened yesterday has nothing to do with what you will do today, Yellow Woman."

"I know—that's what I'm saying—the old stories about the ka'tsina spirit and Yellow Woman can't mean us."

My old grandpa liked to tell those stories best. There is one about Badger and Coyote who went hunting and were gone all day, and when the sun was going down they found a house. There was a girl living there alone, and she had light hair and eyes and she told them that they could sleep with her. Coyote wanted to be with her all night so he sent Badger into a prairie-dog hole, telling him he thought he saw something in it. As soon as Badger crawled in, Coyote blocked up the entrance with rocks and hurried back to Yellow Woman.

"Come here," he said gently.

He touched my neck and I moved close to him to feel his breathing and to hear his heart. I was wondering if Yellow Woman had known who she was—if she knew that she would become part of the stories. Maybe she'd had another name that her husband and relatives called her so that only the ka'tsina from the north and the storytellers would know her as Yellow Woman. But I didn't go on; I felt him all around me, pushing me down into the white river sand.

Yellow Woman went away with the spirit from the north and lived with him and his relatives. She was gone for a long time, but then one day she came back and she brought twin boys.

"Do you know the story?"

"What story?" He smiled and pulled me close to him as he said this. I was afraid lying there on the red blanket. All I could know was the way he felt, warm, damp, his body beside me. This is the way it happens in the stories, I was thinking, with no thought beyond the moment she meets the ka'tsina spirit and they go.

"I don't have to go. What they tell in stories was real only then, back in time immemorial, like they say."

He stood up and pointed at my clothes tangled in the blanket. "Let's go," he said.

I walked beside him, breathing hard because he walked fast, his hand around my wrist. I had stopped trying to pull away from him, because his hand felt cool and the sun was high, drying the river bed into alkali. I will see someone, eventually I will see someone, and then I will be certain that he is only a man—some man from nearby—and I will be sure that I am not Yellow Woman. Because she is from out of time past and I live now and I've been to school and there are highways and pickup trucks that Yellow Woman never saw.

It was an easy ride north on horseback. I watched the change from the cottonwood trees along the river to the junipers that brushed past us in the foothills, and finally there were only piñons, and when I looked up at the rim of the mountain plateau I could see pine trees growing on the edge. Once I stopped to look down, but the pale sandstone had disappeared and the river was gone and the dark lava hills were all around. He touched my hand, not speaking, but always singing softly a mountain song and looking into my eyes.

I felt hungry and wondered what they were doing at home now—my mother, my grandmother, my husband, and the baby. Cooking breakfast, saying, "Where did she go?—maybe kid-naped," and Al going to the tribal police with the details: "She went walking along the river."

The house was made with black lava rock and red mud. It was high above the spreading miles of arroyos and long mesas. I smelled a mountain smell of pitch and buck brush. I stood there beside the black horse, looking down on the small, dim country we had passed, and I shivered.

"Yellow Woman, come inside where it's warm."

TWO

He lit a fire in the stove. It was an old stove with a round belly and an enamel coffeepot on top. There was only the stove, some faded Navajo blankets, and a bedroll and cardboard box. The floor was made of smooth adobe plaster, and there was one small window facing east. He pointed at the box.

"There's some potatoes and the frying pan." He sat on the floor with his arms around his knees pulling them close to his chest and he watched me fry the potatoes. I didn't mind him watching me because he was always watching me—he had been watching me since I came upon him sitting on the river bank trimming leaves from a willow twig with his knife. We ate from the pan and he wiped the grease from his fingers on his Levis.

"Have you brought women here before?" He smiled and kept chewing, so I said, "Do you always use the same tricks?"

"What tricks?" He looked at me like he didn't understand.

"The story about being a ka'tsina from the mountains. The story about Yellow Woman."

Silva was silent; his face was calm.

"I don't believe it. Those stories couldn't happen now," I said.

He shook his head and said softly, "But someday they will talk about us, and they will say, 'Those two lived long ago when things like that happened.' "

He stood up and went out. I ate the rest of the potatoes and thought about things—about the noise the stove was making and the sound of the mountain wind outside. I remembered yesterday and the day before, and then I went outside.

I walked past the corral to the edge where the narrow trail cut through the black rim rock. I was standing in the sky with nothing around me but the wind that came down from the blue mountain peak behind me. I could see faint mountain images in the distance miles across the vast spread of mesas and valleys and plains. I wondered who was over there to feel the mountain wind on those sheer blue edges—who walks on the pine needles in those blue mountains.

"Can you see the pueblo?" Silva was standing behind me. I shook my head. "We're too far away."

"From here I can see the world." He stepped out on the edge. "The Navajo reservation begins over there." He pointed to the east. "The Pueblo boundaries are over here." He looked below us to the south, where the narrow trail seemed to come from. "The Texans have their ranches over there, starting with that valley, the Concho Valley. The Mexicans run some cattle over there too."

"Do you ever work for them?"

"I steal from them," Silva answered. The sun was dropping behind us and shadows were filling the land below. I turned away from the edge that dropped forever into the valleys below.

"I'm cold," I said; "I'm going inside." I started wondering about this man who could speak the Pueblo language so well but who lived on a mountain and rustled cattle. I decided that this man Silva must be Navajo, because Pueblo men didn't do things like that.

"You must be a Navajo."

Silva shook his head gently. "Little Yellow Woman," he said, "you never give up, do you? I have told you who I am. The Navajo people know me, too." He knelt down and unrolled the bedroll and spread the extra blankets out on a piece of canvas. The sun was down, and the only light in the house came from outside—the dim orange light from sundown.

I stood there and waited for him to crawl under the blankets.

"What are you waiting for?" he said, and I lay down beside him. He undressed me slowly like the night before beside the river—kissing my face gently and running his hands up and

down my belly and legs. He took off my pants and then he laughed.

"Why are you laughing?"

"You are breathing so hard."

I pulled away from him and turned my back to him.

He pulled me around and pinned me down with his arms and chest. "You don't understand, do you, little Yellow Woman? You will do what I want."

And again he was all around me with his skin slippery against mine, and I was afraid because I understood that his strength could hurt me. I lay underneath him and I knew that he could destroy me. But later, while he slept beside me, I touched his face and I had a feeling—the kind of feeling for him that overcame me that morning along the river. I kissed him on the forehead and he reached out for me.

When I woke up in the morning he was gone. It gave me a strange feeling because for a long time I sat there on the blankets and looked around the little house for some object of his—some proof that he had been there or maybe that he was coming back. Only the blankets and the cardboard box remained. The .30-30 that had been leaning in the corner was gone, and so was the knife I had used the night before. He was gone, and I had my chance to go now. But first I had to eat, because I knew it would be a long walk home.

I found some dried apricots in the cardboard box, and I sat down on a rock at the edge of the plateau rim. There was no wind and the sun warmed me. I was surrounded by silence. I drowsed with apricots in my mouth, and I didn't believe that there were highways or railroads or cattle to steal.

When I woke up, I stared down at my feet in the black mountain dirt. Little black ants were swarming over the pine needles around my foot. They must have smelled the apricots. I thought about my family far below me. They would be wondering about me, because this had never happened to me before. The tribal police would file a report. But if old Grandpa weren't dead he would tell them what happened—he would laugh and say, "Stolen by a ka'tsina, a mountain spirit. She'll come home—they usually do." There are enough of them to handle things. My mother and grandmother will raise the baby like they raised me. Al will find someone else, and they will go on like before, except that there will be a story about the day I disappeared while I was walking along the river. Silva had come for me; he said he had. I did not decide to go. I just went. Moonflowers blossom in the sand hills before dawn, just as I followed him. That's what I was thinking as I wandered along the trail through the pine trees.

It was noon when I got back. When I saw the stone house I remembered that I had meant to go home. But that didn't seem important any more, maybe because there were little blue flowers growing in the meadow behind the stone house and the gray squirrels were playing in the pines next to the house. The horses were standing in the corral, and there was a beef carcass hanging on the shady side of a big pine in front of the house. Flies buzzed around the clotted blood that hung from the carcass. Silva was washing his hands in a bucket full of water. He must have heard me coming because he spoke to me without turning to face me.

"I've been waiting for you."

"I went walking in the big pine trees."

I looked into the bucket full of bloody water with brown-and-white animal hairs floating in it. Silva stood there letting his hand drip, examining me intently.

"Are you coming with me?"

"Where?" I asked him.

"To sell the meat in Marquez."

"If you're sure it's O.K."

"I wouldn't ask you if it wasn't," he answered.

He sloshed the water around in the bucket before he dumped it out and set the bucket upside down near the door. I followed him to the corral and watched him saddle the horses. Even beside the horses he looked tall, and I asked him again if he wasn't Navajo. He didn't say anything; he just shook his head and kept cinching up the saddle.

"But Navajos are tall."

"Get on the horse," he said, "and let's go."

The last thing he did before we started down the steep trail was to grab the .30-30 from the corner. He slid the rifle into the scabbard that hung from his saddle.

"Do they ever try to catch you?" I asked.

"They don't know who I am."

"Then why did you bring the rifle?"

"Because we are going to Marquez where the Mexicans live."

THREE

The trail leveled out on a narrow ridge that was steep on both sides like an animal spine. On one side I could see where the trail went around the rocky gray hills and disappeared into the southeast where the pale sandrock mesas stood in the distance near my home. On the other side was a trail that went west, and as I looked far into the distance I thought I saw the little town. But Silva said no, that I was looking in the wrong place, that I just thought I saw houses. After that I quit looking off into the distance; it was hot and the wildflowers were closing up their deep-yellow petals. Only the waxy cactus flowers bloomed in the bright sun, and I saw every color that a cactus blossom can be; the white ones and the red ones were still buds, but the purple and the yellow were blossoms, open full and the most beautiful of all.

Silva saw him before I did. The white man was riding a big gray horse, coming up the trail toward us. He was traveling fast and the gray horse's feet sent rocks rolling off the trail into the dry tumbleweeds. Silva motioned for me to stop and we watched the white man. He didn't see us right away, but finally his horse whinnied at our horses and he stopped. He looked at us briefly before he loped the gray horse across the three hundred yards that separated us. He stopped his horse in front of Silva, and his young fat face was shadowed by the brim of his hat. He didn't look mad, but his small, pale eyes moved from the blood-soaked gunny sacks hanging from my saddle to Silva's face and then back to my face.

"Where did you get the fresh meat?" the white man asked.

"I've been hunting," Silva said, and when he shifted his weight in the saddle the leather creaked.

"The hell you have, Indian. You've been rustling cattle. We've been looking for the thief for a long time."

The rancher was fat, and sweat began to soak through his white cowboy shirt and the wet cloth stuck to the thick rolls of belly fat. He almost seemed to be panting from the exertion of talking, and he smelled rancid, maybe because Silva scared him.

Silva turned to me and smiled. "Go back up the mountain, Yellow Woman."

The white man got angry when he heard Silva speak in a language he couldn't understand. "Don't try anything, Indian. Just keep riding to Marquez. We'll call the state police from there."

The rancher must have been unarmed because he was very frightened and if he had a gun he would have pulled it out then. I turned my horse around and the rancher yelled, "Stop!" I looked at Silva for an instant and there was something ancient and dark—something I could feel in my stomach—in his eyes, and when I glanced at his hand I saw his finger on the trigger of the .30-30 that was still in the saddle scabbard. I slapped my horse across the flank and the sacks of raw meat swung against my knees as the horse leaped up the trail. It was hard to keep my balance, and once I thought I felt the saddle slipping backward; it was because of this that I could not look back.

I didn't stop until I reached the ridge where the trail forked. The horse was breathing deep gasps and there was a dark film of sweat on its neck. I looked down in the direction I had come from, but I couldn't see the place. I waited. The wind came up and pushed warm air past me. I looked up at the sky, pale blue and full of thin clouds and fading vapor trails left by jets.

I think four shots were fired—I remember hearing four hollow explosions that reminded me of deer hunting. There could have been more shots after that, but I couldn't have heard them because my horse was running again and the loose rocks were making too much noise as they scattered around his feet.

Horses have a hard time running downhill, but I went that way instead of uphill to the mountain because I thought it was safer. I felt better with the horse running southeast past the round gray hills that were covered with cedar trees and black lava rock. When I got to the plain in the distance I could see the dark green patches of tamaracks that grew along the river; and beyond the river I could see the beginning of the pale sandrock mesas. I stopped the horse and looked back to see if anyone was coming; then I got off the horse and turned the horse around, wondering if it would go back to its corral under the pines on the mountain. It looked back at me for a moment and then plucked a mouthful of green tumbleweeds before it trotted back up the trail with its ears pointed forward, carrying its head daintily to one side to avoid stepping on the dragging reins. When the horse disappeared over the last hill, the gunny sacks full of meat were still swinging and bouncing.

FOUR

I walked toward the river on a wood-hauler's road that I knew would eventually lead to the paved road. I was thinking about waiting beside the road for someone to drive by, but by the time I got to the pavement I had decided it wasn't very far to walk if I followed the river back the way Silva and I had come.

The river water tasted good, and I sat in the shade under a cluster of silvery willows. I thought about Silva, and I felt sad at leaving him; still, there was something strange about him, and I tried to figure it out all the way back home.

I came back to the place on the river bank where he had been sitting the first time I saw him. The green willow leaves that he had trimmed from the branch were still lying there, wilted in the sand. I saw the leaves and I wanted to go back to him—to kiss him and to touch him—but the mountains were too far away now. And I told myself, because I believe it, he will come back sometime and be waiting again by the river.

I followed the path up from the river into the village. The sun was getting low, and I could smell supper cooking when I got to the screen door of my house. I could hear their voices inside—my mother was telling my grandmother how to fix the Jell-o and my husband, Al, was playing with the baby. I decided to tell them that some Navajo had kidnaped me, but I was sorry that old Grandpa wasn't alive to hear my story because it was the Yellow Woman stories he liked to tell best.

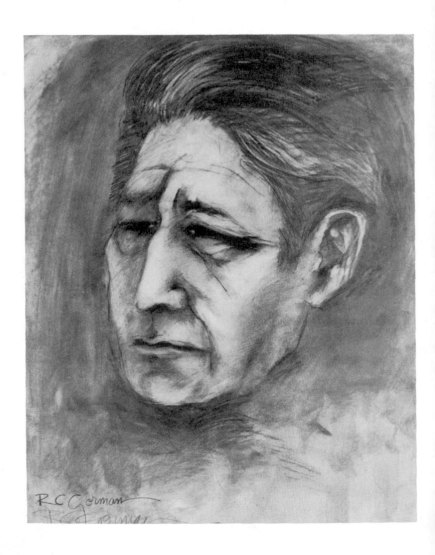

– Simon J. Ortiz

Kaiser
and the War

Kaiser got out of the state pen when I was in the fourth grade. I don't know why people called him Kaiser. Some called him Hitler too, since he was Kaiser, but I don't think he cared at all what they called him. He was probably just glad to get out of the state pen.

Kaiser got into the state pen because he didn't go into the army. That's what my father said anyway, and because he was a crazy nut, according to some people, which was probably why he didn't want to go into the army in the first place, which was what my father said also.

The army wanted him anyway, or maybe they didn't know he was crazy or supposed to be. They came for him out at home on the reservation, and he said he wasn't going to go because he didn't speak good English. Kaiser didn't go to school more than just the first or second grade. He said what he said in Indian and his sister said it in English for him. The army men, somebody from the county draft board, said they'd teach him English, don't worry about it, and how to read and write and give him clothes and money when he got out of the army so that he could start regular as any American. Just like anybody else, and they threw in stuff about how it would be good for our tribe and the people of the U.S.A.

Well, Kaiser, who didn't understand that much English anyway, listened quietly to his sister telling him what the army draft-board men were saying. He didn't ask any questions, just once in a while said, "Yes," like he'd been taught to say in the first grade. Maybe some of the interpretation was lost the way his sister was doing it, or maybe he went nuts like some people said he did once in a while because the next thing he did was to bust out the door and start running for Black Mesa.

The draft-board men didn't say anything at first, and then they got pretty mad. Kaiser's sister cried because she didn't want Kaiser to go into the army, but she didn't want him running out just like that either. She had gone to the Indian school in Albuquerque, and she had learned that stuff about patriotism, duty, honor—even if you were said to be crazy.

At about that time, their grandfather, Faustin, cussed in Indian at the draft-board men. Nobody had noticed when he came into the house, but there he was, fierce-looking as hell as usual, although he wasn't fierce at all. Then he got mad at his granddaughter and the men, asked what they were doing in his house, making the women cry and not even sitting down like friendly people did. Old Faustin and the army confronted each other. The army men were confused and getting more and more nervous. The old man told the girl to go out of the room, and he'd talk to the army himself, although he didn't speak a word of English except "goddammey," which didn't sound too much like English but he threw it in once in a while anyway.

Those army men tried to get the girl to come back, but the old man wouldn't let her. He told her to get to grinding corn or something useful. They tried sign language, and when Faustin figured out what they were waving their hands around for, he laughed out loud. He wouldn't even take the cigarettes offered him, so the army men didn't say anything more. The last thing they did, though, was give the old man a paper, but they didn't try to explain what it was for. They probably hoped it would get read somehow.

Well, after they left, the paper did get read by the girl, and she told Faustin what it was about. The law was going to come and take Kaiser to jail because he wouldn't go into the army by himself. Grandfather Faustin sat down and talked quietly to himself for a while and then he got up to look for Kaiser.

Kaiser was on his way home by then, and his grandfather told him what was going to happen. They sat down by the side of the road and started to make plans. Kaiser would go hide up on Black Mesa and maybe go up all the way to Brushy Mountain if the law really came to poking around seriously. Faustin would take him food and tell him the news once in a while.

Everybody in the village knew what was going on pretty soon. Some approved, and some didn't. Some thought it was pretty funny. My father, who couldn't go in the army even if he wanted to because there were too many of us kids, laughed about it for days. The people who approved of it and thought it funny were the ones who knew Kaiser was crazy and that the army must be even crazier. The ones who disapproved were mostly those who were scared of him. A lot of them were the parents or brothers of girls who they must have suspected of liking Kaiser. Kaiser was pretty good-looking and funny in the way he talked for a crazy guy. And he was a hard worker. He worked every day out in the fields or up at the sheep camp for his parents while they were alive and for his sister and nephew and grandfather. These people, who were scared of him and said he should have gone into the army perhaps it'll do him good, didn't want him messing around their daughters or sisters, which they said he did from time to time. Mostly these people were scared he would do *something*, and there was one too many nuts around in the village anyway, they said.

My old man didn't care though. He was buddies with Kaiser. When there was a corn dance up at the community hall they would have a whole lot of fun singing and laughing and joking, and once in a while when someone brought around a bottle or two they would really get going and the officers of the tribe would have to warn them to behave themselves.

Kaiser was O.K., though. He came around home quite a lot. His own kinfolks didn't care for him too much because he was crazy, and they didn't go out of their way to invite him to eat or spend the night when he dropped by their homes and it happened to get dark before he left. My mother didn't mind him around. When she served him something to eat, she didn't act like he was nuts, or supposed to be; she just served him and fussed over him like he was a kid, which Kaiser acted like a lot of the time. I guess she didn't figure a guy who acted like a kid was crazy.

Right after we finished eating, if it happened to be supper, my own grandfather, who was a medicine man, would talk to him and to all of us kids who were usually paying only half attention. He would tell us advice, about how the world was, how each person, everything, was important. And then he would tell us stories about the olden times. Legends mostly, about the ka'tsina, Spider Woman, where our *hano,* people, came from. Some of the stories were funny, some sad, and some pretty boring. Kaiser would sit there, not saying anything except *"Eheh,"* which is what you're supposed to say once in a while to show that you're listening to the olden times.

After half of us kids were asleep, Grandfather would quit talking, only Kaiser wouldn't want him to quit and he'd ask for more, but Grandfather wouldn't tell any more. What Kaiser would do was start telling himself about the olden times. He'd

lie on the floor in the dark, or sometimes up on the roof which was where he'd sleep in the summer, talking. And sometimes he'd sing, which is also part of the old times. I would drift off to sleep just listening to him.

Well, he didn't come around home after he went up on Black Mesa. He just went up there and stayed there. The law, which was the County Sheriff, an officer, and the Indian Agent from the Indian Affairs office in Albuquerque, came out to get him, but nobody would tell them where he was. The law had a general idea where he was, but that didn't get them very far because they didn't know the country around Black Mesa. It's rougher than hell up there, just a couple of sheep camps in a lot of country.

The Indian Agent had written a letter to the officers of the tribe that they would come up for Kaiser on a certain day. There were a lot of people waiting for them when they drove up to the community meeting hall. The County Sheriff had a bulging belly and he had a six-shooter strapped to his hip. When the men standing outside the community hall saw him step out of the government car, they made jokes. Just like the Lone Ranger, someone said. The law didn't know what they were laughing about, and they said, Hello, and paid no attention to what they couldn't understand.

Faustin was among them. But he was silent and he smoked a roll-your-own. The Agent stopped before him, and Faustin took a slow drag on his roll-your-own but didn't look at the man.

"Faustin, my old friend," the Agent said. "How are you?"

The old man didn't say anything. He let the tobacco smoke out slowly and looked straight ahead. Someone in the crowd told Faustin what the Agent had said, but the old man didn't say anything at all.

The law thought he was praying or that he was a wise man contemplating his answer, the way he was so solemn-like, so they didn't press him. What Faustin was doing was ignoring the law. He didn't want them to talk with him. He turned to a man at his side.

"Tell this man I do not want to talk. I can't understand what they're saying in American anyway. And I don't want anyone to tell me what they say. I'm not interested." He looked at the government then, and he dismissed their presence with his indignation.

"The old man isn't gonna talk to you," someone said.

The Agent and Sheriff Big Belly glared at the man. "Who's in charge around here?" the Sheriff said.

The Indians laughed. They joked by calling each other big belly. The Governor of the tribe and two chiefs came soon. They greeted the law, and then they went into the meeting hall to confer about Kaiser.

"Well, have you brought Kaiser?" the Indian Agent asked, although he saw that they hadn't and knew that they wouldn't.

"No," the Governor said. And someone interpreted for him. "He will not come."

"Well, why don't you bring him? If he doesn't want to come, why don't you bring him. A bunch of you can bring him," the Agent said. He was becoming irritated.

The Governor, chiefs, and men talked to each other. One old man held the floor a while, until others got tired of him telling about the old times and how it was and how the Americans had said a certain thing and did another and so forth. Someone said, "We can bring him. Kaiser should come by himself anyway. Let's go get him." He was a man who didn't like Kaiser. He looked around carefully when he got through speaking and sat down.

"Tell the Americans that is not the way," one of the chiefs said. "If our son wants to meet these men he will come." And the law was answered with the translation.

"I'll be a son-of-a-bitch," the Sheriff said, and the Indians laughed quietly. He glared at them and they stopped. "Let's go get him ourselves," he continued.

The man who had been interpreting said, "He is crazy."

"Who's crazy?" the Sheriff yelled, like he was refuting an accusation. "I think you're all crazy."

"Kaiser, I think he is crazy," the interpreter said like he was ashamed of saying so. He stepped back, embarrassed.

Faustin then came to the front. Although he said he didn't want to talk with the law, he shouted. "Go get Kaiser yourself. If he's crazy, I hope he kills you. Go get him."

"O.K.," the Agent said when the interpreter finished. "We'll go get him ourselves. Where is he?" The Agent knew no one would tell him, but he asked it anyway.

With that, the Indians assumed the business that the law came to do was over, and that the law had resolved what it came to do in the first place. The Indians began to leave.

"Wait," the Agent said. "We need someone to go with us. He's up on Black Mesa, but we need someone to show us where."

The men kept on leaving. "We'll pay you. The government will pay you to go with us. You're deputized," the Agent said. "Stop them, Sheriff," he said to the County Sheriff, and the Sheriff yelled, "Stop, come back here," and put a hand to his six-shooter. When he yelled, some of the Indians looked at him to laugh. He sure looked funny and talked funny. But some of them came back. "All right, you're deputies, you'll get paid," the Sheriff said. Some of them knew what that meant, others weren't too sure. Some of them decided they'd come along for the fun of it.

The law and the Indians piled into the government car and a pickup truck which belonged to one of the deputies who was assured that he would get paid more than the others.

Black Mesa is fifteen miles back on the reservation. There are dirt roads up to it, but they aren't very good; nobody uses them except sheepherders and hunters in the fall. Kaiser knew what he was doing when he went up there, and he probably saw them when they were coming. But it wouldn't have made any difference, because when the law and the deputies came up to the foot of the mesa they still weren't getting anywhere. The deputies, who were still Indians, wouldn't tell or didn't really know where Kaiser was at the moment. So they sat for a couple of hours at the foot of the mesa, debating what should be done. The law tried to get the deputies to talk. The Sheriff was boiling mad by this time, getting madder too, and he was for *persuading* one of the deputies into telling where Kaiser was exactly. But he reasoned the deputy wouldn't talk, being that he was Indian too, and so he shut up for a while. He had figured out why the Indians laughed so frequently even though it was not as loud as before they were deputized.

Finally, they decided to walk up Black Mesa. It's rough going, and when they didn't know which was the best way to go up they found it was even rougher. The real law dropped back one by one to rest on a rock or under a piñon tree until only the deputies were left. They watched the officer from the Indian Affairs office sitting on a fallen log some yards back. He was the last one to keep up so far, and he was unlacing his shoes. The deputies waited patiently for him to start again and for the others to catch up.

"It's sure hot," one of the deputies said.

"Yes, maybe it'll rain soon," another said.

"No, it rained for the last time last month. Maybe next year."

"Snow then," another said.

They watched the Sheriff and the Indian Agent walking toward them half a mile back. One of them limped.

"Maybe the Americans need a rest," someone said. "We walked a long ways."

"Yes, they might be tired," another said. "I'll go tell that one that we're going to stop to rest," he said, and walked back to the law sitting on the log. "We gonna stop to rest," he told the law. The law didn't say anything as he massaged his feet. And the deputy walked away to join the others.

They didn't find Kaiser that day or the next day. The deputies said they could walk all over the mesa without finding him for all eternity, but they wouldn't find him. They didn't mind walking, they said. As long as they got paid for their time. Their crops were already in, and they'd just hire someone to haul winter wood for them now that they had the money. But they refused to talk. The ones who wanted to tell where Kaiser was, if they knew, didn't say so out loud, but they didn't tell anyway so it didn't make any difference. They were too persuaded by the newly found prosperity of employment.

The Sheriff, exhausted by the middle of the second day of walking the mesa, began to sound like he was for going back to Albuquerque. Maybe Kaiser'd come in by himself; he didn't see any sense in looking for some Indian anyway just to get him into the army. Besides, he'd heard the Indian was crazy. When the Sheriff had first learned the Indian's name was Kaiser he couldn't believe it, but he was assured that wasn't his real name, just something he was called because he was crazy. But the Sheriff didn't feel any better or less tired, and he was getting jumpy about the crazy part.

At the end of the second day, the law decided to leave. Maybe we'll come back, they said. We'll have to talk this over with the Indian Affairs officials. Maybe it'll be all right if that Indian doesn't have to be in the army after all. And they left. The Sheriff, his six-shooter off his hip now, was pretty tired out, and he didn't say anything.

The officials for the Indian Affairs didn't give up though. They sent back some more men. The County Sheriff had decided it wasn't worth it; besides, he had a whole county to take care of. And the Indians were deputized again. More of them volunteered this time; some had to be turned away. They had figured out how to work it: they wouldn't have to tell, if they knew, where Kaiser was. All they would have to do was walk and say from time to time, "Maybe he's over there by that canyon. Used to be there was some good hiding places back when the Apache and Navajo were raising hell." And some would go over there and some in the other direction, investigating good hiding places. But after camping around Black Mesa for a week this time, the Indian Affairs gave up. They went by Faustin's house the day they left for Albuquerque and left a message: the government would wait, and when Kaiser least expected it, they would get him and he would have to go to jail.

Kaiser decided to volunteer for the army. He had decided to after he had watched the law and the deputies walk all over the mesa. Grandfather Faustin had come to visit him up at one of the sheep camps, and the old man gave him all the news at home, and then he told Kaiser the message the government had left.

"O.K.," Kaiser said. And he was silent for a while and nodded his head slowly like his grandfather did. "I'll join the army."

"No," his grandfather said. "I don't want you to. I will not allow you."

"Grandfather, I do not have to mind you. If you were my grandfather or uncle on my mother's side, I would listen to you and probably obey you, but you are not, and so I will not obey you."

"You are really crazy then," Grandfather Faustin said. "If

that's what you want to do, go ahead." He was angry and he was sad, and he got up and put his hand on his grandson's shoulder and blessed him in the people's way. After that the old man left. It was evening when he left the sheep camp, and he walked for a long time away from Black Mesa before he started to sing.

The next day, Kaiser showed up at home. He ate with us, and after we ate we sat in the living room with my grandfather.

"So you've decided to go into the Americans' army," my grandfather said. None of us kids, nor even my parents, had known he was going, but my grandfather had known all along. He probably knew as soon as Kaiser had walked into the house. Maybe even before that.

My grandfather blessed him then, just like Faustin had done, and he talked to him of how a man should behave and what he should expect. Just general things, and Grandfather turned sternly toward us kids, who were playing around as usual. My father and mother talked with him too, and when they were through, my grandfather put corn meal in Kaiser's hand for him to pray with. Our parents told us kids to tell Kaiser good-bye and good luck, and after we did he left.

The next thing we heard was that Kaiser was in the state pen.

Later on, some people went to visit him up at the state pen. He was O.K. and getting fat, they said, and he was getting on O.K. with everybody, the warden told them. And when someone had asked Kaiser if he was O.K., he said he was fine and he guessed he would be American pretty soon, being that he was around them so much. The people left Kaiser some home-baked bread and dried meat and came home after being assured by the warden that he'd get out pretty soon, maybe right after the war. Kaiser was a model inmate. When the visitors got home to the reservation, they went and told Faustin his grandson was O.K., getting fat and happy as any American. Old Faustin didn't have anything to say about that.

Well, the war was over after a while. Faustin died sometime near the end of it. Nobody had heard him mention Kaiser at all. Kaiser's sister and nephew were the only ones left at their home. Sometimes someone would ask about Kaiser, and his sister or nephew would say, "Oh, he's fine. He'll be home pretty soon. Right after the war." But after the war was over, they just said he was fine.

My father and a couple of other guys went down to the Indian Affairs office to see what they could find out about Kaiser. They were told that Kaiser was going to stay in the pen longer now because he had tried to kill somebody. Well, he just went crazy one day, and he made a mistake, so he'll just have to stay in for a couple of more years or so, the Indian Affairs said. That was the first anybody heard of Kaiser trying to kill somebody, and some people said why the hell didn't they put him in the army for that like they wanted to in the first place. So Kaiser remained in the pen long after the war was over, and most of the guys who had gone into the army from the tribe had come home. When he was due to get out, the Indian Affairs sent a letter to the Governor, and several men from the village went to get him.

My father said Kaiser was quiet all the way home on the bus. Some of the guys tried to joke with him, but he just wouldn't laugh or say anything. When they got off the bus at the highway and began to walk home, the guys broke into song, but that didn't bring Kaiser around. He kept walking quiet and reserved in his gray suit. Someone joked that Kaiser probably owned the only suit in the whole tribe.

"You lucky so-and-so. You look like a rich man," the joker said. The others looked at him sharply and he quit joking, but Kaiser didn't say anything.

When they reached his home, his sister and nephew were very happy to see him. They cried and laughed at the same time, but Kaiser didn't do anything except sit at the kitchen table and look around. My father and the other guys gave him advice and welcomed him home again and left.

After that, Kaiser always wore his gray suit. Every time you saw him he was wearing it. Out in the fields or at the plaza watching the *katzina,* he wore the suit. He didn't talk much any more, my father said, and he didn't come around home any more, either. The suit was getting all beat-up looking, but he just kept on wearing it so that some people began to say that he was showing off.

"That Kaiser," they said, "he's always wearing his suit, just like he was an American or something. Who does he think he is anyway?" And they'd snicker, looking at Kaiser with a sort of envy. Even when the suit was torn and soiled so that it hardly looked anything like a suit, Kaiser wore it. And some people said, "When he dies, Kaiser is going to be wearing his suit." And they said that like they wished they had gotten a suit like Kaiser's.

Well, Kaiser died, but without his gray suit. He died up at one of his distant relative's sheep camps one winter. When someone asked about the suit, they were told by Kaiser's sister that it was rolled up in some newspaper at their home. She said that Kaiser had told her, before he went up to the sheep camp, that she was to send it to the government. But, she said, she couldn't figure out what he meant, whether Kaiser had meant the law or somebody, maybe the state pen or the Indian Affairs.

The person who asked about the suit wondered about this Kaiser's instructions. He couldn't figure out why Kaiser wanted to send a beat-up suit back. And then he figured, Well, maybe that's the way it was when you either went into the state pen or the army and became an American.

– R. C. Gorman

Nowhere to Go

On Highway 66, east of Holbrook, Arizona, stood a lone hitchhiker. He had long hair and he was Indian. Navajo. He was young. About twenty-two.

A white boy in navy uniform stopped for him, and the Indian hopped into the automobile without a word. He had no luggage. "Where you heading, man?" the boy in uniform asked.

"Gallup," answered the Navajo.

After riding several minutes without speaking, the boy in uniform asked, "You Indian, ain't you?"

"Yeah."

"Apache?" the white boy pressed.

"Navajo."

Several more minutes passed. The Indian remained silent until the white boy asked another question. "Where you coming from?"

"Alcatraz."

"Alcatraz!" The white boy lit up. "That's in San Francisco where the Indians are trying to take over, ain't it?"

"Yeah."

"You live on a reservation?"

61

"Yeah." The Indian seemed uninterested.

"What do you do on a reservation?"

"Nothing." The Indian seemed even more uninterested.

"Why did you go to Alcatraz?"

"It was something to do."

"Why did you leave?"

"I guess I saw what I wanted."

The two travelers remained silent for several miles. The white boy grew restless from the silence and spoke up again. "I'm on my way to Georgia, off on leave. It's quite a ways more to go just listening to myself and the radio. I've got quite a ways more to go. And you sure don't talk much."

The Navajo smiled and reached into his jacket and brought out a bottle of cheap wine. "I haven't warmed up. It's cold out there. Have a drink, buddy." The navy man took several swigs, and so did the Navajo.

"The Apaches and the Navajos," began the navy man cautiously, "do they get along? I mean do they care for each other?"

"They used to be one people," answered the Indian. "That's what they tell me," he added, as if to say that he couldn't care less.

"Oh, yeah? How?"

The Navajo thought for a minute, offered the white boy another shot of wine, and took a great gulp himself.

"Well," he began, somewhat deliberating how to start his story properly. "Well, in *those* days the Apaches and the Navajos roamed as one people. Except that the tribes were divided up into several clans."

"What's a clan?" interrupted the white boy.

"Well, I guess it's like small families all living together. Related and unrelated. The clans determine whether you can fuck or marry a girl or make jokes with her or leave her alone entirely. If a girl is related to your clan she is like your own sister or mother, even if you've never seen each other in your life."

"So what the hell does that have to do with the fucking Apaches and Navajos?" the white boy asked anxiously.

"Well, the so-called Apache group never could get along with the Navajo bunch. They were fucking clans but they preferred to fight each other instead."

"Fight!" The navy man laughed out loud. "No shit?"

"Oh, yeah. But it was all in a game. They took their fighting seriously but in a great fun way. Many braves were killed."

The boy from the navy thought about this for a moment and decided another shot of the wine would clear his mind a bit. He reached over for the bottle and took a swig. "What was so much fun about fighting and killing each other? I'd settle for a good fuck anyday."

"Sure, but war was a game with them. In wars—like when they fought the Spaniards and other Indians—they did it often just to test their strength and also to make certain gains."

"Gains?" asked the white boy after another gulp of wine.

"Like women and horses and food. But mostly they did it just to show how fucking strong they were. When there was no Spanish marching through their land to fight, or other Indians around to throw a scare into, they would turn on each other. Just for the practice. In a fun way."

"Shit. O.K., what do you mean by a fun way?"

"Well, they would fight and kill each other all day, and when it came time to chow down someone would announce, 'Let's stop this bullshit for now. Time to eat.' And they would all march home to their camps and have a great feast with each other or their families or whatever. And then they would fuck all night and have a good time. In the morning someone would announce, 'After the dead braves have been removed from yesterday's meeting, let's all march to that dry arroyo four miles east of here where the sand is clean and white and continue our game.' And one of the braves would always say, 'That will be fun!' "

"Oh shit!" the white boy laughed. "Give me another swig and I'll believe you, man. I'll believe anything you tell me."

Both men laughed, and the Indian cleared his throat to continue his story, which he now seemed to derive more interest from as the wine bottle reached the halfway mark. "And so, after the time and place had been set, they'd meet and continue their matches. Men died right and left, and the clean white sand turned spotted with red blood. And when the men got hungry and horny again they would call it a day and march home satisfied with the day's game."

"Oh, shit! Give me the bottle, you fucker."

They finished off the bottle and threw it out of the car window. And the Indian spoke again. "Well, after many months of fighting the tribe grew smaller and smaller until many women had to sleep alone or with each other. And so they, too, started to quarrel and fight each other, but for a different kind of fun. Meantime, I don't know where the busy old wise leaders of the tribe were all this time, but suddenly they realized one day what was happening. The young men of the tribe were killing themselves off! 'We are going to be no more,' the wise men said. 'What can be done?' they asked each other. And after many more meetings they found a solution. It was decided that the Apache clan group would move north of the Jemez River, and the Navajo clan group would move south of the Jemez River. And never play fun games with each other again. So they did. And to this day they are separated by that river. That's my story."

They rode for several more miles and finally came into the town of Gallup. "I'll get off at the next stoplight," the Indian said.

"Where will you go?" the white boy asked.

"Shit," the Indian answered, and looked about him as if he were surveying his private town. "There's always a place to stay for an Indian here. Even the Anglos welcome you. They have a busy jail for Indians. This is no missionary town. Indians and tourists are its prey to keep alive. Not Jesus."

"By the way, you didn't mention how the Navajos gained back what they had lost."

"That's another story, man," answered the Navajo.

The sailor winked at the young Navajo. "As an Anglo," he said, "can I offer you a place to stay tonight? We can share another bottle and you can tell me the rest of the story."

The Indian smiled and extended his hand for a shake. "Sure, why not? I have nowhere to go."

– Joseph Little

Impressions on Turning Wombward

California is nine hundred miles and two and one half hours away. The fact is of little consequence. My head hurts, and the taste of bile coats my dry mouth. From my slumped position in one of the airport lounge chairs, I pass judgment on all the scurrying people. It is like sitting in an exclusive bus station. The people are just as strange, only dressed better. Jet engines hum in my head. My eyes sting from the glare of the sun coming in through the wall of windows, and my stomach continues to contract.

After a thousand miles it is always the last half mile that commands my full attention. There is the bar, a squat cinder-block building with two dark windows and a narrow door. Its outer walls are covered with the Hamms bear and huge glasses of foaming beer. On weekends cars cluster around it as western music blares at them through an outside speaker with just enough amplification to muffle the garbled mouthings and induced conviviality within. There is the house with the oversize television antenna on its roof, and the oversize grotto on its wall: black rock with a statue of the Blessed Virgin nestled in the center. There is the general store, very small and very quiet, existing for paydays. There is the big white sign hanging from a green pole stationed at the side of the road. Cut like a policeman's badge, it bears the words in bold, black letters: INDIAN RESERVATION. Then there is home.

The bus hisses to a stop, the loose gravel along the edge of the road making a crunching sound under the wheels. The doors click open, and my feet touch the ground.

Before me stands the small, wooden frame house, almost hidden by a row of piñon trees. The long open porch partly hides the rusty, corrugated tin roof that slopes at a sharp pitch. The crumbling brick chimney that sits comically and precariously on its tin incline breathes no smoke. A large hill covered with scrub brush rises behind the house and makes it seem smaller than it actually is. The door is open.

Summer jobs are a way to kill time. The workday starts early with a quick, tasteless breakfast, a cold morning that one never becomes accustomed to, and a truck that starts only with coaxing. The base of operations is a fenced-in lot which shelters trucks and construction equipment. It holds three secondhand, 1952 Studebaker dump trucks, a discarded army flatbed, a couple of pickup trucks, a dilapidated road sweeper with U.S. AIR FORCE still stenciled on its side, and a brand new road grader. It takes awhile to get used to the mingled fumes of gas, oil, and diesel fuel.

The lot is half an hour's drive from the work site which is located down the throat of a long, narrow canyon. By the time the sun has struggled over the rim of the canyon, the steady, powerful, surging growl of power saws and the uneven chopping of axes can be heard amplified through the winding canyon. Trees are felled, cut, and the pitch-sticky blocks hauled away. Rest periods mean a leisurely smoked cigarette, a drink of water, a joke or two, and a sly story exchanged between the older workers. Taut muscles get a chance to relax, and perspiration can become cool and welcome. The magnified racket gives way to a magnified silence. Talk quickly drifts into the upper branches of the trees, where it mingles with the fickle wind and is lost. White, blue, and green become sharp hues as the clouds lazily traverse the strip of sky that spans the canyon's ridges. The graceful outline of a hawk draws you upward until you master the gentle air currents and float effortlessly, light and free.

By the time we return to the lot, dusk has not yet set in. The day has already given up, but the sun still hangs reluctantly above the horizon. The men depart in twos and threes. Dinner is waiting.

Dinners are functional. One indulges in them. But it is the evenings that tantalize. These I devour greedily. They are cool, subdued, and inviting. Like sleep and women, they are to be yielded to. They whisper your thoughts as you lie on your back, grass beneath you and a detached, haunting black void above you. You feel and think with no perceptible distinction between the two functions. Your whole body rolls backward over memory's subtly undulating slopes: the trees that toppled in slow motion, the woodchuck that scurried through the grass, the loud guffaws that exploded with the punch line of a new joke. There were the clouds, the trees, the hills, the last days of school, and the longing memory of home.

–Leslie Silko

Tony's Story

ONE

It happened one summer when the sky was wide and hot and the summer rains did not come; the sheep were thin, and the tumbleweeds turned brown and died. Leon came back from the army. I saw him standing by the Ferris wheel across from the people who came to sell melons and chili on San Lorenzo's Day. He yelled at me, "Hey Tony—over here!" I was embarrassed to hear him yell so loud, but then I saw the wine bottle with the brown-paper sack crushed around it.

"How's it going, buddy?"

He grabbed my hand and held it tight like a white man. He was smiling. "It's good to be home again. They asked me to dance tomorrow—it's only the Corn Dance, but I hope I haven't forgotten what to do."

"You'll remember—it will all come back to you when you hear the drum." I was happy, because I knew that Leon was once more a part of the pueblo. The sun was dusty and low in the west, and the procession passed by us, carrying San Lorenzo back to his niche in the church.

"Do you want to get something to eat?" I asked.

Leon laughed and patted the bottle. "No, you're the only

69

one who needs to eat. Take this dollar—they're selling hamburgers over there." He pointed past the merry-go-round to a stand
with cotton candy and a snow-cone machine.

It was then that I saw the cop pushing his way through the
crowds of people gathered around the hamburger stand and
bingo-game tent; he came steadily toward us. I remembered
Leon's wine and looked to see if the cop was watching us; but he
was wearing dark glasses and I couldn't see his eyes.

He never said anything before he hit Leon in the face with
his fist. Leon collapsed into the dust, and the paper sack floated
in the wine and pieces of glass. He didn't move and blood kept
bubbling out of his mouth and nose. I could hear a siren. People
crowded around Leon and kept pushing me away. The tribal
policemen knelt over Leon, and one of them looked up at the
state cop and asked what was going on. The big cop didn't
answer. He was staring at the little patterns of blood in the dust
near Leon's mouth. The dust soaked up the blood almost before
it dripped to the ground—it had been a very dry summer. The
cop didn't leave until they laid Leon in the back of the paddy
wagon.

The moon was already high when we got to the hospital in
Albuquerque. We waited a long time outside the emergency
room with Leon propped between us. Siow and Gaisthea kept
asking me, "What happened, what did Leon say to the cop?"
and I told them how we were just standing there, ready to buy
hamburgers—we'd never even seen him before. They put
stitches around Leon's mouth and gave him a shot; he was
lucky, they said—it could've been a broken jaw instead of
broken teeth.

TWO

They dropped me off near my house. The moon had moved
lower into the west and left the close rows of houses in long

shadows. Stillness breathed around me, and I wanted to run from the feeling behind me in the dark; the stories about witches ran with me. That night I had a dream—the big cop was pointing a long bone at me—they always use human bones, and the whiteness flashed silver in the moonlight where he stood. He didn't have a human face—only little, round, white-rimmed eyes on a black ceremonial mask.

Leon was better in a few days. But he was bitter, and all he could talk about was the cop. "I'll kill the big bastard if he comes around here again," Leon kept saying.

With something like the cop it is better to forget, and I tried to make Leon understand. "It's over now. There's nothing you can do."

I wondered why men who came back from the army were troublemakers on the reservation. Leon even took it before the pueblo meeting. They discussed it, and the old men decided that Leon shouldn't have been drinking. The interpreter read a passage out of the revised pueblo law-and-order code about possessing intoxicants on the reservation, so we got up and left.

Then Leon asked me to go with him to Grants to buy a roll of barbed wire for his uncle. On the way we stopped at Cerritos for gas, and I went into the store for some pop. He was inside. I stopped in the doorway and turned around before he saw me, but if he really was what I feared, then he would not need to see me—he already knew we were there. Leon was waiting with the truck engine running almost like he knew what I would say.

"Let's go—the big cop's inside."

Leon gunned it and the pickup skidded back on the highway. He glanced back in the rear-view mirror. "I didn't see his car."

"Hidden," I said.

Leon shook his head. "He can't do it again. We are just as good as them."

The guys who came back always talked like that.

THREE

The sky was hot and empty. The half-grown tumbleweeds were dried-up flat and brown beside the highway, and across the valley heat shimmered above wilted fields of corn. Even the mountains high beyond the pale sandrock mesas were dusty blue. I was afraid to fall asleep so I kept my eyes on the blue mountains—not letting them close—soaking in the heat; and then I knew why the drought had come that summer.

Leon shook me. "He's behind us—the cop's following us!"

I looked back and saw the red light on top of the car whirling around, and I could make out the dark image of a man, but where the face should have been there were only the silvery lenses of the dark glasses he wore.

"Stop, Leon! He wants us to stop!"

Leon pulled over and stopped on the narrow gravel shoulder.

"What in the hell does he want?" Leon's hands were shaking.

Suddenly the cop was standing beside the truck, gesturing for Leon to roll down his window. He pushed his head inside, grinding the gum in his mouth; the smell of Doublemint was all around us.

"Get out. Both of you."

I stood beside Leon in the dry weeds and tall yellow grass that broke through the asphalt and rattled in the wind. The cop studied Leon's driver's license. I avoided his face—I knew that I couldn't look at his eyes, so I stared at his black half-Wellingtons, with the black uniform cuffs pulled over them; but my eyes kept moving, upward past the black gun belt. My legs were quivering, and I tried to keep my eyes away from his. But it was like the time when I was very little and my parents warned me

not to look into the masked dancers' eyes because they would
grab me, and my eyes would not stop.

"What's your name?" His voice was high-pitched and it
distracted me from the meaning of the words.

I remember Leon said, "He doesn't understand English so
good," and finally I said that I was Antonio Sousea, while my
eyes strained to look beyond the silver frosted glasses that he
wore; but only my distorted face and squinting eyes reflected
back.

And then the cop stared at us for a while, silent; finally he
laughed and chewed his gum some more slowly. "Where were
you going?"

"To Grants." Leon spoke English very clearly. "Can we go
now?"

Leon was twisting the key chain around his fingers, and I
felt the sun everywhere. Heat swelled up from the asphalt and
when cars went by, hot air and motor smell rushed past us.

"I don't like smart guys, Indian. It's because of you
bastards that I'm here. They transferred me here because of
Indians. They thought there wouldn't be as many for me here.
But I find them." He spit his gum into the weeds near my foot
and walked back to the patrol car. It kicked up gravel and dust
when he left.

We got back in the pickup, and I could taste sweat in my
mouth, so I told Leon that we might as well go home since he
would be waiting for us up ahead.

"He can't do this," Leon said. "We've got a right to be on
this highway."

I couldn't understand why Leon kept talking about
"rights," because it wasn't "rights" that he was after, but Leon
didn't seem to understand; he couldn't remember the stories
that old Teofilo told.

I didn't feel safe until we turned off the highway and I

could see the pueblo and my own house. It was noon, and everybody was eating—the village seemed empty—even the dogs had crawled away from the heat. The door was open, but there was only silence, and I was afraid that something had happened to all of them. Then as soon as I opened the screen door the little kids started crying for more Kool-Aid, and my mother said "no," and it was noisy again like always. Grandfather commented that it had been a fast trip to Grants, and I said "yeah" and didn't explain because it would've only worried them.

"Leon goes looking for trouble—I wish you wouldn't hang around with him." My father didn't like trouble. But I knew that the cop was something terrible, and even to speak about it risked bringing it close to all of us; so I didn't say anything.

That afternoon Leon spoke with the Governor, and he promised to send letters to the Bureau of Indian Affairs and to the State Police Chief. Leon seemed satisfied with that. I reached into my pocket for the arrowhead on the piece of string.

"What's that for?"

I held it out to him. "Here, wear it around your neck—like mine. See? Just in case," I said, "for protection."

"You don't believe in *that,* do you?" He pointed to a .30-30 leaning against the wall. "I'll take this with me whenever I'm in the pickup."

"But you can't be sure that it will kill one of them."

Leon looked at me and laughed. "What's the matter," he said, "have they brainwashed you into believing that a .30-30 won't kill a white man?" He handed back the arrowhead. "Here, you wear two of them."

FOUR

Leon's uncle asked me if I wanted to stay at the sheep camp for a while. The lambs were big, and there wouldn't be much for

me to do, so I told him I would. We left early, while the sun was still low and red in the sky. The highway was empty, and I sat there beside Leon imagining what it was like before there were highways or even horses. Leon turned off the highway onto the sheep-camp road that climbs around the sandstone mesas until suddenly all the trees are piñons.

Leon glanced in the rear-view mirror. "He's following us!"

My body began to shake and I wasn't sure if I would be able to speak. "There's no place left to hide. It follows us everywhere."

Leon looked at me like he didn't understand what I'd said. Then I looked past Leon and saw that the patrol car had pulled up beside us; the piñon branches were whipping and scraping the side of the truck as it tried to force us off the road. Leon kept driving with the two right wheels in the rut—bumping and scraping the trees. Leon never looked over at it so he couldn't have known how the reflections kept moving across the mirror-lenses of the dark glasses. We were in the narrow canyon with pale sandstone close on either side—the canyon that ended with a spring where willows and grass and tiny blue flowers grow.

"We've got to kill it, Leon. We must burn the body to be sure."

Leon didn't seem to be listening. I kept wishing that old Teofilo could have been there to chant the proper words while we did it. Leon stopped the truck and got out—he still didn't understand what it was. I sat in the pickup with the .30-30 across my lap, and my hands were slippery.

The big cop was standing in front of the pickup, facing Leon. "You made your mistake, Indian. I'm going to beat the shit out of you." He raised the billy club slowly. "I like to beat Indians with this."

He moved toward Leon with the stick raised high, and it was like the long bone in my dream when he pointed it at me—a human bone painted brown to look like wood, to hide what it really was; they'll do that, you know—carve the bone into a spoon and use it around the house until the victim comes within range.

The shot sounded far away and I couldn't remember aiming. But he was motionless on the ground and the bone wand lay near his feet. The tumbleweeds and tall yellow grass were sprayed with glossy, bright blood. He was on his back, and the sand between his legs and along his left side was soaking up the dark, heavy blood—it had not rained for a long time, and even the tumbleweeds were dying.

"Tony! You killed him—you killed the cop!"

"Help me! We'll set the car on fire."

Leon acted strange, and he kept looking at me like he wanted to run. The head wobbled and swung back and forth, and the left hand and the legs left individual trails in the sand. The face was the same. The dark glasses hadn't fallen off and they blinded me with their hot-sun reflections until I pushed the body into the front seat.

The gas tank exploded and the flames spread along the underbelly of the car. The tires filled the wide sky with spirals of thick black smoke.

"My God, Tony. What's wrong with you? That's a state cop you killed." Leon was pale and shaking.

I wiped my hands on my Levis. "Don't worry, everything is O.K. now, Leon. It's killed. They sometimes take on strange forms."

The tumbleweeds around the car caught fire, and little heatwaves shimmered up toward the sky; in the west, rain clouds were gathering.

–*Simon J. Ortiz*

A Story
of Ríos and
Juan Jesús

Ríos bought a car one day. This was down in San Juan.

He used to save his money off Annie and Rita. They worked down on Calle Luna. Sorta dumb, but pretty, and they liked Ríos.

José Ríos, soldier of misfortune for sure, he belonged in the looney. He used to say to me, Let's go visit Juan Jesús.

One day, first time I met him, sitting outside barracks which used to be a convent, he say, You wanna go visit Juan Jesús? I don't know who Juan Jesús is. John Jesus, man, says Ríos. I don't know John Jesus by that name either. That's him calling for help or something. And along with the tree frogs and hi-fi going in dayroom, some godawful screaming about something. The world's caving in, Ríos say. You wanna go closer to listen to John Jesus scream? So we move closer, under tall palm trees by the hospital, and listen to John Jesus screaming his lungs inside out. Sounds like it comes from the trees, the green coconuts, that evening. I think that Ríos is gonna tell me Juan Jesús is trapped in the coconuts. The tree frogs, goddamn them, don't even stop chirping away. I be a son-of-a-bitch, says Ríos.

So I say this time, Okeydokey. And we go walk over

the hospital, up some stairs, down hall, more stairs, two, three flights, and medic mopping hall floor says, Where you guys going anyway? Upstairs, Ríos tells him. And PFC medic, that's all he wants to know, I guess, goes back to mopping. More stairs, and we listen for Juan Jesús to welcome us or guide us or tell us close-up what he is trying to tell the world. But silence, a NO ADMITTANCE sign on door with little window and wire inside glass.

The door don't move when Ríos push. Hey, Juan Jesús, shout Ríos, goddoggit. Juan Jesús, the hall thunders. Then somebody begins to moan and cry. That's not Juan Jesús, Ríos say softly. Shut up you nut, José Ríos say almost like pleading. And then there's the godawful scream.

Goddamnit, Juan Jesús, what you tryna say? Ríos shouts. The medics come and curse at us. Get out of here. We'll call the MPs, for chrissake, don't you have any sense, they tell us. The MPs we don't like, so we begin to leave. You come back and we'll put you there with them, the clean medics say confidently and push us down the stairs. The only guy, Ríos, who wants to see what Juan Jesús is saying, gets push down the stairs.

Anyway, Ríos bought a car.

You want to go see the girls, sisters, I know them, come on, have supper and sleep. Come on, Indian, Ríos says. I can't, I say. I heard he never had a car before, don't know what it looks like, don't know if he can drive, and the traffic is worse than murder in San Juan, so I say, I got a guard duty tonight. So Ríos go by himself. And later I sit under the palm trees and listen and think that Juan Jesús is locked up tight in a green coconut.

The next day, Ríos says to me, You damn Indians, you got some sense. And I smile to see what he means, but he just laughs and don't say nothing. So I suspect and ask around what he means. What he means was he busted all four tires off his car. I ask him. He says, Yeah, goddamn curb. We laugh about it.

So one night, late night, Puerto Rican style, calm and damp, little kids tired all from play baseball in street asleep and dreaming, Annie and Rita on Calle Luna still tricking but tired by now, they—musta been the MPs or medics or the C.O.—heard him yelling up at Juan Jesús. Hey, Juan Jesús, goddammit shut up, you don't say things like that. They ain't no such thing. Hush up, man.

Along with the screams of Juan Jesús, they heard him. What you doing, Ríos? they ask sternly. He was to tell Juan Jesús not to talk like that. You better go to bed, Ríos, they said. Yessir, he said, but he was listening to Juan Jesús. But after a while, Juan Jesús don't make no more sound.

Ríos didn't even bother about his car, he just let it sit by the curb. Don't need a car, he said to me. He was thinking of what Juan Jesús say. He's afraid, he's pissed off, Ríos said. And then quietly. He shouldn't talk like that. And that night he was shouting up at Juan Jesús again, giving him talk, Don't say those things, you goddamn pork chop anyway. I'm your friend and the Indian is your friend.

The MPs heard him again, and this time, with all due consideration and after the medics gave him tests, the C.O. signed the papers and they put Ríos up there with Juan Jesús.

Chapter I

Johonah-eh peeked through the loose feathered clouds the wind had scattered free. His copper–gold face tinted the yellow flowers on the chamisas that grew well in the thirsty land of Arizona. The light from his smile gave life to shadows that hid from gray clouds. The strength in his touch brought warmth and encouraged gentle smiles on the faces of those people below.

They had long waited for this day. It had been the first in many years that their crops had not been destroyed by drought, insects, or even soldiers. Many days had been spent planting, caring for small fields of corn, squash, watermelons, and pumpkins. The people had done all this secretly, hidden by the great red walls of Canyon de Chelly. Only two or three people would go at one time to the fields to tend to the crops. They were always very cautious and suspicious of those who came too close to their tiny fields, for there were, at that time, rumors of soldiers in the area.

The people worked hastily preparing for a feast. Much time had gone into this celebration since they had decided they were

82

safe. Maybe it was the brightness of Johonah-eh on those peaceful late October afternoons, when the winds danced gracefully across the canyon floor. Maybe it was the weariness of the people, maybe they were tired of running from soldiers, and maybe they needed something to make them laugh. Maybe it was all these things. Whatever the reason, they were having a feast.

Besides, had it not been said that "Rope Thrower," the one whom the *belliconas* called Kit Carson, was being criticized about his method of warfare against the people? Even his own chiefs were finding fault with his technique of dealing with the people. For he'd never actually been able to bring the people out to fight openly. Instead, he went about destroying their sources of food, eventually forcing them into submission by starvation. Whether or not that was the reason for the little activity on his part in the past few weeks, the people were beginning to feel a faint hope of making it through the winter. And it would very definitely be another hard winter; all of nature said so.

It seemed like forever to Natanii since he had felt solid food in his stomach. He watched his mother in the distance, expecting her to call very soon to come and eat. In all his seven years he had known only fear and hunger. Now, with the air filled with smells of meat and bread, his stomach became impatient and growled for attention.

Looking about at some of the people eating in the shelter of dark green junipers, he wondered how all this came about. Silently he asked himself why the people were hungry all the time. He asked himself about the fear they lived with daily. His great dark eyes that claimed most of his face flashed from the earth to the clouds that lived in the sky, begging for an answer. But if the clouds knew, they gave no sign and ignored him.

Welcome sounds of laughter from a nearby family brought his eyes to the squash they ate and woke up the hunger that slept inside of him. Finally his mother called to him. "Eat," she said softly. She carried bread in her arms and held a battered container. As she came toward him, its contents spilled from side to side. Finding a place of smooth red rock and fine red sand, they settled down to wait for Natanii's grandfather. Natanii could see him making his way toward them, his gray hair flying in the wind. He was slow in coming, for old age, not thinking much of time, held him back. Natanii's mother, sensing that her son was anxious to begin, pulled out warm meat and squash and urged him to begin. Natanii ate rapidly. It had been many days since he had had more than a thin piece of bread at one time. He ate so much so quickly that his stomach became almost sick. His mother, realizing this, pushed him gently against a large red rock that sat behind him and told him to wait for his stomach and food to settle.

His grandfather had finally arrived and started to eat when Natanii heard his mother speak of soldiers. It seemed to Natanii that they were always talking about the soldiers. Half listening to their conversation, he studied each carefully. He examined every detail that came to sight and all their words that came to mind. With frank admiration for both, he decided that he was glad they were his family. Besides them, he had only one uncle whom he did not know well. He could not really think of him as a part of the family.

His mother was a happy young woman, he thought. As happy as one could be under the circumstances they lived with daily. He found no unpleasantness in looking at her; in fact she was quite pretty, although she now looked a little tired from all the morning work. A strand of loose, black hair hung over her smooth cheek, and she pushed it back from time to time. Somehow it made her appear much younger than her twenty-two years.

Placing her hands below each ear, she drew her head

forward slowly and at the same time moved her hands backward, catching the stray wisps of hair in her long fingers. As her slim fingers gracefully retied the string that held her hair together in the back of her neck, Natanii noticed the silver bracelet that hugged her small wrist. The bracelet that gleamed like daylight had once been his father's. Natanii thought often of him. And always when the face of his father came to visit in Natanii's mind, his eyes became warm and stung until the water of his tears washed away the loneliness and the face of his father.

A little more than a year ago, when the people were again fleeing the soldiers, Natanii's father went with a group of men to hold off the soldiers at a pass in the canyon. While they did this, the remainder of the people successfully made their way to the base of the mountains. Later this small group of men also made their way to the mountains, but Natanii's father was one of those who remained in the desolate canyon. Life had been pushed out of his strong body by the big guns fired by the soldiers. The people told Natanii that his father had been a very brave man. He died a hero's death, they said.

After that, Natanii's grandfather exercised most of the authority in the family. He comforted his grandson and his daughter by telling them that his son's death was given by his son in exchange for the lives of his family. Being a medicine man, his grandfather was learned in the ways of life. He gave Natanii much in the endless stories he told. With his grandfather's powerful beliefs to console him, Natanii finally came to accept his father's death. He even began to understand that if he were to live, someone else must die. That was one of the rules set down by the holy ones, the Yeis, and the people honored those rules.

Natanii had spent much time in thought, trying to understand the Yeis. There were many strict laws, and understanding came slowly when talk of soldiers rang loud in his ears.

According to his grandfather and all the old ones, after First Man and First Woman were created from two ears of corn, they were told that they would always live within the land between the four sacred mountains and that only the natural barriers of the river gorges and mountain ranges would limit their wanderings. Natanii could not remember when he first heard this story, but if it were true, why then were there soldiers who carried guns and chased the people from their homes and changed their way of life?

The wind had become cool and blew sand in Natanii's frowning face, as if to take away the worry and play with him. Thoughtfully he chewed on more bread, and its taste warmed him. His grandfather, through with his meal, watched him, questioning the quiet of him. The old one worried about the young one. Natanii had lately grown too old for his age, and it somehow seemed wrong.

To interrupt the little one's disturbing thoughts, his grandfather said, "Natanii, go and gather wood for the fire." Immediately Natanii's strong legs carried him swiftly into the beginning of another canyon that promised more firewood than the empty one which now hid his mother. A small cornfield came into view, and he stopped to admire it. Picking up forgotten kernels of colored corn, he studied the field. He could see that the corn stalks had turned from the light-green colors to faded yellows. As he walked closer to the middle of the field he noticed the crinkly sounds that came from husks that lay everywhere. He was impressed by the height of the stalks. They grew taller than Natanii. Far off he heard his grandfather calling for the wood. Making his way between the rows of dry corn stalks, he finally reached the clearing. As he walked away he thought to himself that with all those steep cliffs to hide it, no one, not even the soldiers, would be able to find it. He began gathering loose pieces of wood that were lying about. When his

arms became tired and refused to hold any more, he started
back.

As he neared camp, he thought he heard children crying.
The closer he came, the louder the crying. People were talking in
hushed, upset voices. His short steps quickened as he turned in
the direction of the crowd to investigate. Suddenly, from the
mouth of the canyon came loud popping noises that echoed in
other canyons. Natanii knew those sounds well. Gunfire! All
around him came the thunder of rifles. His first thought was of
his grandfather, and he started for him but was knocked down
by people running for cover. The wood he held tumbled in the
four directions when he hit the ground. He didn't know why, but
he tried to gather those logs that lay near him once more. Then
he got up and tried to run, but found it hard to move. The full
meal in his stomach made his legs lazy.

He had gone only a little way before he fell once more, face
down, pushed by a horse. He fell on top of the wood and one of
the sharp sticks pierced his arm. He pushed himself upon his
knees and looked at the blue-eyed rider on the horse. The man
was raising his sword, aiming for his target. His target was
Natanii. Natanii's heart drummed loudly, singing of fear. He
moved his small hands over the earth and jumped up. When the
horse came for him again, as Natanii knew it would, his short
brown arms lifted two handfuls of dirt into the horse's face. The
horse reared and staggered backward, and the soldier disappeared into the midst of dust. Natanii stood waiting for the dust
to settle. The taste of fine red clay was heavy in his mouth. His
arm ached a little and he checked it to see how badly it was cut.
Someone bumped into him and he looked up. The people were
running all around, trying to gather a few of their belongings
before getting away.

Natanii ran searching for his grandfather only to find him

lying in the red sand, dead. He had tried to protect his family in
the only way he could. Knowing his grandfather as he did,
Natanii guessed that he had fallen in the middle of a prayer for
protection. His left hand still held the sacred pollen bag and
near his right hand lay a stone ax, a powerful protection symbol.
Nayenezgani, "Monster Slayer," one of the twins in Navajo
religion, used the ax ceremonially for protection. It worked for
him, they say, but Natanii's grandfather lay alone in an arroyo
partially covered by the dark red flesh of Mother Earth.

Although he hated to leave his grandfather's side, his fear of
the pale men in uniform was great, and he ran for cover. Not too
far from him grew thick young junipers. He moved desperately
for the protection they offered and wrapped himself in the
prickly green blankets of numerous stems and boughs.

He stayed there for the remainder of the day, cautiously
watching, quietly sitting, barely daring to breathe. His eyes kept
finding his grandfather in the distance, and his ears became
lonesome for the music of his grandfather's voice. His heart
knew that his grandfather preferred to find death in this way.
Many times he was not pleased with old age. He felt he might be
a burden to his family and requested to be left alone in a canyon
with some water and food to wait quietly and with dignity for
death.

Natanii's mother felt that the old one's time was near. She
also felt sure he knew it. Others before him had been known to
predict their deaths in the same manner. Natanii had heard of
other grandfathers and grandmothers who had passed on in the
lonely canyons in the old days when the people were few and the
enemy were many. When an old one knew his weak body could
mean the very life or death of the people and so elected to
remain alone. "How many canyons, how many grandfathers?"
Natanii asked himself.

Forcing himself to turn his head in another direction,

Natanii saw that the battle was almost over. During the entire fight, he did not see his mother at all. He checked those people on the ground and found that she was not among them. He knew well the faces of those that lay everywhere. His young mind could not believe or understand that they would move no more.

A small cluster of men, women, and children had come together in the defenseless open space of the battleground, trying to protect themselves by grouping together. The young ones were in the middle, the men and women on the outside. But this seemed only to make a game for those on horses. Two or three would ride threateningly at the helpless people on foot. The people, trying to avoid the deadly riders, would scatter everywhere. They would quickly regroup in another part of the canyon, pushing the little ones to the center, only to have the horses charge at them again. The men on horses played this game a long time, Natanii thought. For some reason, the whole thing reminded Natanii of the days when he had helped his grandfather clear patches of land for small cornfields. His grandfather would choose a certain place for the fields. Then he, with the help of Natanii, would make a fire. The wind would blow in the direction that the field would be. Soon the whole area would be empty. Watching the bloody scene, Natanii decided the horses could have been the wind and the people on foot could have been the bushes and tumbleweeds. The people, like the bushes and weeds, would soon disappear. Natanii didn't know why he thought of this but he did, and he was ashamed of making the comparison.

The men on horses were beginning to tire of their game. Eventually it all came to the same end with more of the people scattered on the ground. The weaker people fell quickly. They were easy targets for the powerful horses. The stronger ones made the game last longer for those on horses. But finally even those people fell, if not from the horses' speed then from the bullets that came from the guns that rode the horses. Seeing so many fall from the same source, it came to Natanii's mind of all the times he and other children had played a game of life and death. They had chased each other with make-believe guns. But these men played no game. They carried real guns.

Now that the battle had quieted down, the silence was strange and uncomfortable. The smell of burning cornfields filled the canyon. Those in uniform began to talk among themselves. They hobbled their horses for the remainder of day. The food Natanii's mother had diligently fixed and then left behind, the men in uniform enjoyed. Walking about destroying all that they did not want for souvenirs, or things they could not take with them, they came near the bushes that cared for Natanii. Too near, he thought. Worrying in a way he'd never done before, he closed his eyes and waited to be discovered. Somehow the ones in uniform did not notice him. He relaxed a little. Knowing that he would not be able to leave in the light of day, he unconsciously checked Johonah-eh's place in the sky. It would not be too long before he would be able to leave. In his heart he thanked the junipers. He ignored his cramped position and tried not to move when the needles on the stems pushed him away. Later he tried to make himself more comfortable, but the junipers would not let him. He continued to watch fearfully.

The large meal in his stomach could have surely put him to sleep had it not also reminded him of other natural functions that he could not control. After a serious struggle with himself, he forced away the uncomfortable and unwanted feeling.

Checking once more on the men who surrounded him and satisfied that he would not be discovered, Natanii placed his heavy head on two dusty, tired knees. He folded thin arms around skinny legs and listened to the wind's mournful song. It sang to Natanii of that long, long day.

– Leslie Silko

Uncle Tony's Goat

W_e had a hard time finding the right kind of string to use. We knew we needed gut to string our bows the way the men did, but we were little kids and we didn't know how to get any. So Kenny went to his house and brought back a ball of white cotton string that his mother used to string red chili with. It was thick and soft and it didn't make very good bowstring. As soon as we got the bows made we sat down again on the sand bank above the stream and started skinning willow twigs for arrows. It was past noon, and the tall willows behind us made cool shade. There were lots of little minnows that day, flashing in the shallow water, swimming back and forth wildly like they weren't sure if they really wanted to go up or down the stream; it was a day for minnows that we were always hoping for—we could have filled our rusty coffee cans and old pickle jars full. But this was the first time for making bows and arrows, and the minnows weren't much different from the sand or the rocks now. The secret is the arrows. The ones we made were crooked, and when we shot them they didn't go straight—they flew around in arcs and curves; so we crawled through the leaves and branches, deep into the willow groves, looking for the best, the straightest

93

willow branches. But even after we skinned the sticky wet bark from them and whittled the knobs off, they still weren't straight. Finally we went ahead and made notches at the end of each arrow to hook in the bowstring, and we started practicing, thinking maybe we could learn to shoot the crooked arrows straight.

We left the river, each of us with a handful of damp, yellow arrows and our fresh-skinned willow bows. We walked slowly and shot arrows at bushes, big rocks, and the juniper tree that grows by Pino's sheep pen. They were working better just like we had figured; they still didn't fly straight, but now we could compensate for that by the way we aimed them. We were going up to the church to shoot at the cats old Sister Julian kept outside the cloister. We didn't want to hurt anything, just to have new kinds of things to shoot at.

But before we got to the church we went past the grassy hill where my uncle Tony's goats were grazing. A few of them were lying down chewing their cud peacefully, and they didn't seem to notice us. The billy goat was lying down, but he was watching us closely like he already knew about little kids. His yellow goat eyes didn't blink, and he stared with a wide, hostile look. The grazing goats made good deer for our bows. We shot all our arrows at the nanny goats and their kids; they skipped away from the careening arrows and never lost the rhythm of their greedy chewing as they continued to nibble the weeds and grass on the hillside. The billy goat was lying there watching us and taking us into his memory. As we ran down the road toward the church and Sister Julian's cats, I looked back, and my uncle Tony's billy goat was still watching me.

My uncle and my father were sitting on the bench outside the house when we walked by. It was September now, and the farming was almost over, except for bringing home the melons and a few pumpkins. They were mending ropes and bridles and feeling the afternoon sun. We held our bows and arrows out in front of us so they could see them. My father smiled and kept braiding the strips of leather in his hands, but my uncle Tony put down the bridle and pieces of scrap leather he was working on and looked at each of us kids slowly. He was old, getting some white hair—he was my mother's oldest brother, the one that scolded us when we told lies or broke things.

"You'd better not be shooting at things," he said, "only at rocks or trees. Something will get hurt. Maybe even one of you."

We all nodded in agreement and tried to hold the bows and arrows less conspicuously down at our sides; when he turned back to his work we hurried away before he took the bows away from us like he did the time we made the slingshot. He caught us shooting rocks at an old wrecked car; its windows were all busted out anyway, but he took the slingshot away. I always wondered what he did with it and with the knives we made ourselves out of tin cans. When I was much older I asked my mother, "What did he ever do with those knives and slingshots he took away from us?" She was kneading bread on the kitchen table at the time and was probably busy thinking about the fire in the oven outside. "I don't know," she said; "you ought to ask him yourself." But I never did. I thought about it lots of times, but I never did. It would have been like getting caught all over again.

The goats were valuable. We got milk and meat from them. My uncle was careful to see that all the goats were treated properly; the worst scolding my older sister ever got was when my mother caught her and some of her friends chasing the newborn kids. My mother kept saying over and over again, "It's a good thing I saw you; what if your uncle had seen you?" and even though we kids were very young then, we understood very well what she meant.

The billy goat never forgot the bows and arrows, even after

the bows had cracked and split and the crooked, whittled arrows were all lost. This goat was big and black and important to my uncle Tony because he'd paid a lot to get him and because he wasn't an ordinary goat. Uncle Tony had bought him from a white man, and then he'd hauled him in the back of the pickup all the way from Quemado. And my uncle was the only person who could touch this goat. If a stranger or one of us kids got too near him, the mane on the billy goat's neck would stand on end and the goat would rear up on his hind legs and dance forward trying to reach the person with his long, spiral horns. This billy goat smelled bad, and none of us cared if we couldn't pet him. But my uncle took good care of this goat. The goat would let Uncle Tony brush him with the horse brush and scratch him around the base of his horns. Uncle Tony talked to the billy goat—in the morning when he unpenned the goats and in the evening when he gave them their hay and closed the gate for the night. I never paid too much attention to what he said to the billy goat; usually it was something like "Get up, big goat! You've slept long enough," or "Move over, big goat, and let the others have something to eat." And I think Uncle Tony was proud of the way the billy goat mounted the nannies, powerful and erect with the great black testicles swinging in rhythm between his hind legs.

We all had chores to do around home. My sister helped out around the house mostly, and I was supposed to carry water from the hydrant and bring in kindling. I helped my father look after the horses and pigs, and Uncle Tony milked the goats and fed them. One morning near the end of September I was out feeding the pigs their table scraps and pig mash; I'd given the pigs their food, and I was watching them squeal and snap at each other as they crowded into the feed trough. Behind me I could hear the milk squirting into the eight-pound lard pail that Uncle Tony used for milking.

When he finished milking he noticed me standing there; he motioned toward the goats still inside the pen. "Run the rest of them out," he said as he untied the two milk goats and carried the milk to the house.

I was seven years old, and I understood that everyone, including my uncle, expected me to handle more chores; so I hurried over to the goat pen and swung the tall wire gate open. The does and kids came prancing out. They trotted daintily past the pigpen and scattered out, intent on finding leaves and grass to eat. It wasn't until then I noticed that the billy goat hadn't come out of the little wooden shed inside the goat pen. I stood outside the pen and tried to look inside the wooden shelter, but it was still early and the morning sun left the inside of the shelter in deep shadow. I stood there for a while, hoping that he would come out by himself, but I realized that he'd recognized me and that he wouldn't come out. I understood right away what was happening and my fear of him was in my bowels and down my neck; I was shaking.

Finally my uncle came out of the house; it was time for breakfast. "What's wrong?" he called out from the door.

"The billy goat won't come out," I yelled back, hoping he would look disgusted and come do it himself.

"Get in there and get him out," he said as he went back into the house.

I looked around quickly for a stick or broom handle, or even a big rock, but I couldn't find anything. I walked into the pen slowly, concentrating on the darkness beyond the shed door; I circled to the back of the shed and kicked at the boards, hoping to make the billy goat run out. I put my eye up to a crack between the boards, and I could see he was standing up now and that his yellow eyes were on mine.

My mother was yelling at me to hurry up, and Uncle Tony was watching. I stepped around into the low doorway, and the goat charged toward me, feet first. I had dirt in my mouth and up my nose and there was blood running past my eye; my head ached. Uncle Tony carried me to the house; his face was stiff with anger, and I remembered what he'd always told us about animals: they won't bother you unless you bother them first. I didn't start to cry until my mother hugged me close and wiped my face with a damp wash rag. It was only a little cut above my eyebrow, and she sent me to school anyway with a Band-Aid on my forehead.

Uncle Tony locked the billy goat in the pen. He didn't say what he was going to do with the goat, but when he left with my father to haul firewood, he made sure the gate to the pen was wired tightly shut. He looked at the goat quietly and with sadness; he said something to the goat, but the yellow eyes stared past him.

"What's he going to do with the goat?" I asked my mother before I went to catch the school bus.

"He ought to get rid of it," she said. "We can't have that goat knocking people down for no good reason."

I didn't feel good at school. The teacher sent me to the nurse's office and the nurse made me lie down. Whenever I closed my eyes I could see the goat and my uncle, and I felt a stiffness in my throat and chest. I got off the school bus slowly, so the other kids would go ahead without me. I walked slowly and wished I could be away from home for a while. I could go over to Grandma's house, but she would ask me if my mother knew where I was and I would have to say no, and she would make me go home first to ask. So I walked very slowly, because I didn't want to see the black goat's hide hanging over the corral fence.

When I got to the house I didn't see a goat hide or the goat, but Uncle Tony was on his horse and my mother was standing beside the horse holding a canteen and a flour sack bundle tied with brown string. I was frightened at what this meant. My uncle looked down at me from the saddle.

"The goat ran away," he said. "Jumped out of the pen somehow. I saw him just as he went over the hill beyond the river. He stopped at the top of the hill and he looked back this way."

Uncle Tony nodded at my mother and me and then he left; we watched his old roan gelding splash across the stream and labor up the steep path beyond the river. Then they were over the top of the hill and gone.

Uncle Tony was gone for three days. He came home early on the morning of the fourth day, before we had eaten breakfast or fed the animals. He was glad to be home, he said, because he was getting too old for such long rides. He called me over and looked closely at the cut above my eye. It had scabbed over good, and I wasn't wearing a Band-Aid any more; he examined it very carefully before he let me go. He stirred some sugar into his coffee.

"That goddamn goat," he said. "I followed him for three days. He was headed south, going straight to Quemado. I never could catch up to him." My uncle shook his head. "The first time I saw him he was already in the piñon forest, halfway into the mountains already. I could see him most of the time, off in the distance a mile or two. He would stop sometimes and look back." Uncle Tony paused and drank some more coffee. "I stopped at night. I had to. He stopped too, and in the morning we would start out again. The trail just gets higher and steeper. Yesterday morning there was frost on top of the blanket when I woke up and we were in the big pines and red oak leaves. I couldn't see him any more because the forest is too thick. So I turned around." Tony finished the cup of coffee. "He's probably in Quemado by now."

I thought his voice sounded strong and happy when he said

this, and I looked at him again, standing there by the door, ready to go milk the nanny goats. He smiled at me.

"There wasn't ever a goat like that one," he said, "but if that's the way he's going to act, O.K. then. That damn goat got pissed off too easy anyway."

– Simon J. Ortiz

The Killing
of a State Cop

Felipe was telling me how it happened. I was then twelve years old. They would get him, he knew, he said. And he was scared. He looked around nervously all the time that we sat on the trough which ran around the water tank.

Felipe wasn't a bad guy. Not at all. A little wild maybe. He had been in the marines and he could have gotten kicked out if he had wanted to, he said. But he hadn't because he could play it pretty straight like a good guy, too.

He used to tell me a lot of things, about what he had seen, about what he had done, about what he planned to do, and about what other people could do to you. That was one trouble with him. He was always thinking about what other people could do to you. Not the people around our place, the Indians, but other people.

How that state policeman died was like this (Felipe wanted me to remember what he said always, and he talked very seriously and sometimes sadly, and again he said they would get him anyway):

"What the hell. He deserved to die, the bastard."

It was the wine, Felipe said. And that thing he had about people, I guess. He didn't say, but I knew.

"It makes you warm in the head and other things like that," he said.

He had gone to town from the reservation with Antonio, his brother. They drove their pickup truck to town where they bought the wine from a bootlegger. "From some stupid Mexican bartender. Geesus, I hate Mexicans."

Felipe spat on the ground. Indians were not supposed to drink or buy liquor at that time. It was against the law. Felipe hated the law and broke it whenever he felt he could get away with it.

"One time in Winslow I got off the train when it stopped at the depot and walked into a bar next to the depot to buy a beer. I was still in the marines then and in uniform. This barman, he looked at me very mean and asked if I was Indian. 'Shore,' I said. And he told me to get the hell out before he called the cops. Goddamn, I hated that, and I went around the back and peed on the back door. I don't know why, just because I hated him, I guess."

———

Felipe and his brother were walking in town, not saying anything much, and maybe looking at things they wanted to buy when they had the money. They stopped in front of the Golden Theater and looked at the pictures of what was in the movies that day and the next day.

"Hey, Indio. Hey, what hell you doing?" It was Luis Baca, a member of the state police who patrolled the state highway near the reservation.

The brothers hated the man. Felipe regarded him with a fierce hate because he had been thrown in jail by him once. He had been beaten, and he feared the cop because of that. They did not answer.

"Hey, goddammey Indio, get the hell away from there. Get out of town."

For no reason at all.

"For no reason at all. Goddamn, I got mad and I called him a dirty, fat, lazy good-for-nothing, ugly Mexican."

Felipe looked around him and told me I better learn to be something more than him, a guy who would probably die in the electric chair up at Santa Fe.

Felipe told Antonio he was going to kill the Mexican, but Antonio said that it was no good talk and persuaded him to leave town.

They left, followed by the curses and jeers of Luis Baca. When they got back to the pickup truck, they opened another bottle of wine and drank.

"It makes a noise in your head, and you want to do something," Felipe told me.

They decided to go home. Almost out of town, they heard a siren scream behind them and saw a black police car with Baca driving it. Felipe told Antonio not to stop. They did not go faster, though. Luis Baca drove alongside and laughed at the brothers, who were frightened and suspicious.

Antonio stepped on the brake then, and he let the policeman pass them. They were past the town limits.

"Antonio, my brother, he is a kind of a funny guy," Felipe said. "He doesn't get mad like me. I mean yell or cuss. He just kind of looks mean or sad. He told me to give him the wine and he drank some and put it on the seat between his legs."

The police car leading and pickup truck following were heading toward the reservation.

Suddenly, a few miles out of town, Antonio pressed his foot

down on the gas pedal and the pickup truck picked up speed. It seemed that the policeman did not see the truck bearing down on him until it was almost too late.

"Antonio wasn't trying to run into the car. I thought he was going to, but he was only trying to scare the bastard."

Luis Baca swerved off the road anyway, and there was a cloud of dust as his car skidded into a shallow ditch.

Felipe and Antonio didn't stop. Looking through the rear window, they saw the cop get out of the car. Antonio stopped the pickup truck. He started up again and made a U-turn. Passing by the police car, they saw that the policeman was trying to get his car out. The tires kept spinning and throwing gravel. A few miles down the road, they turned around and headed back toward the police car again.

"Wine makes you do stupid things. Son-of-a-bitch. Sometimes you think about putting your hand between a girl's legs or taking money from somebody or even killing somebody."

They slowed down as they approached the police car. It was slowly coming out of the ditch.

"I drank the wine left in the bottle, and as we passed I threw the bottle against the window of the car and I made a dirty sign with my hand at the Mexican," Felipe said.

Antonio speeded the truck up. They kept looking back, and soon they saw the police car following them and heard the siren. They turned into the road that led into the reservation. It was a dirt road, and the truck bounced and jolted as they sped along it. The police car turned off the highway and followed them.

Felipe reached behind the seat of the truck and brought out a .30-30 Winchester rifle which was wrapped in a homemade case of denim from old Levis. He took the rifle out of the denim case and pulled down the lever so that the chamber was open. There was nothing in there, and he closed the lever and lowered the hammer very carefully as usual. He opened the truck compartment and brought out an almost full box of cartridges.

"You remember that .30-30 I was using when I went deer hunting last year? The one I let you shoot even though you aren't supposed to before you shoot at a deer with it. That one. My father bought it when he was working for the railroad. That one."

They followed the road that led to the village, but turned off to another road before they got there. The road climbed a hill and led toward Black Mesa, several miles to the south. At the top of the hill they stopped and watched to see if the police car was still following them. It was at the bottom of the hill and coming up.

The dirt road led through a forest of juniper and piñon. This was near the heart of the reservation. They sped by a scattered herd of sheep tended by a boy who looked at them as they passed by. The sheep dogs barked at them and ran alongside for a while.

"The road is very rough and sometimes sandy, and we couldn't go too fast. No one uses it except sheepherders and people going for wood in their wagons. We stopped on a small hill to see if Luis Baca was still coming after us. We couldn't see him because of the forest, so I told my brother to shut off the engine so I could listen. It was real quiet in the forest like it always is, and you can hear things from a long ways away. I could hear the cop car still coming, about a half-mile back. I told Antonio to go on."

They passed the windmill which was a mile from Black Mesa. The one road branched there into several directions. The one that led east of Black Mesa into some rough country and canyons was the one they chose.

Antonio slowed the truck and drove slowly until they saw that the policeman could see which road they had taken, and then he speeded up again.

"Aiee, I can see stupidity in a man. Sometimes even my own. I can see a man's drunkenness making him do crazy things. And Luis Baca, a very stupid son-of-a-bitch, was more than I could see. He wanted to die. And I, because I was drunken and *muy loco* like a Mexican friend I had from Nogales used to say about me when we would play with the whores in Korea and Tokyo, wanted to make him die. I did not care for anything else except that Luis Baca who I hated was going to die."

Directly to the east of Black Mesa is a plain which runs for about two miles in all directions. There is grass on the plain, and there are many prairie dogs. At the edge of the grassy plain is a thin forest of juniper and piñon. A few yards beyond the edge of the forest there is a deep ravine which is the tail end of a deep and wide canyon which runs from the east toward Black Mesa. The ravine comes to a point almost against one edge of Black Mesa. There is only a narrow passage, which crumbles away each year with erosion, between the ravine and the abruptly rising slopes of the mesa. The road passes this point and goes around the mesa and to a spring called Spider Spring.

The brothers passed through the narrow passage and stopped fifty yards away. Felipe got out with the rifle and bullets, and Antonio parked the pickup truck behind a growth of stunted juniper growing thickly together.

"I took some bullets out of the box and put them into the rifle. Six of them, I think, the kind with soft points. I laid down the rifle for a while and waited for Antonio. He didn't come right away from the truck and I called to him. We laid down behind a small mound of sand and rocks; the ground was hot from the sun. We could hear the police car coming.

" 'Are we just going to scare him so he won't bother us no more?' Antonio asked me.

"I looked at Antonio, and he looked like he used to when

we were kids and he used to pretend not to be scared of rattle-snakes.

"'I don't know,' I said. I was going to shoot the man. I don't know why, but I was going to. Maybe I was kind of scared then.

"When the car came out of the trees, it was not coming very fast. It approached the narrow place and slowed down. I thought Luis Baca would see me, so I slid down until I could barely see over the edge of the mound behind which we lay.

"He had slowed down because of the narrow place, and I thought he would stop and turn back. But he didn't. He shifted into first and came on very slowly. That's when I put my rifle on a flat rock and aimed it. Right at the windshield where the steering wheel is. The sun was shining on the windshield very brightly and I could not see very well."

Felipe relaxed a bit, took a breath, opened and closed the lever on the rifle.

The bullet made a hole right above where the metal and glass were joined by a strip of rubber in front of the steering wheel. It made an irregular pattern in the windshield glass. The shot echoed back and forth in the ravine and was followed by another shot. The bullet made a hole a few inches to the upper right of the first. Another shot followed and it was wild. It ricocheted off the top and into some rocks on the mesa slope.

"Four times I shot, and I could see the holes almost in the spot where I wanted them to be. One wasn't though. But the car didn't stop or go crooked. It kept coming and crossed the narrow place. It stopped then, and Luis Baca got out very slowly. He called something like he was crying. *'Compadre,'* he said. He held up his right hand and reached to us. There was blood on his neck and shoulder."

Felipe settled himself into place and aimed very carefully.

Luis Baca tried to unbuckle his pistol belt, but the bullet tore into his belly and he leaned against the car as he was knocked back a step. A last shot whipped his head around violently, and he dropped to the ground. Felipe started to put more bullets into the rifle but decided not to.

The two brothers walked to the car and stood over the still-moving body of Luis Baca. Antonio reached down and slid the police revolver out of the holster, took aim, and pulled the trigger.

"Luis Baca, the poor fool, made a feeble gurgle like a sick cat and went to hell.

"They will catch me, I know. There were people who saw us being chased by the cop. Antonio went to Albuquerque and he took the pistol. He will get caught too."

That was what he told me that night when we were sitting at the water tank. He used to tell me all kinds of things because I would listen. I liked those stories he told about the Korean war. That was where he learned how to drive a truck, and he had saved up his money so that he could buy a truck after he got out of the marines. Felipe and I used to go hunting and fishing too.

I sort of believed him, about the killing of Luis Baca the state cop, but not really, until a few days later when I heard my mother talking about it with my father. I asked something about it, and they told me to forget it and said that Felipe would probably die in the electric chair. Every night, for quite a while, I prayed a rosary or something for him.

– Opal Lee Popkes

Zuma Chowt's Cave

In 1903 an Indian named Chowt followed a pack of rats through Dume Canyon, north of Santa Monica. To Chowt, the wind-scarred canyon was not Dume Canyon (a white-man name) but was called Huyat, something white people would have laughed at had they known its meaning.

But the white man chasing Chowt was less interested in the terrain than in proving his superiority to a fleeing Indian. Chowt had learned devious methods of avoiding capture. He tried to tell them the truth. He was following a rat, which was the truth. The white man stopped chasing, and sat down to laugh so long and hard that Chowt escaped and continued to follow the trail of the rat.

Chowt did not particularly care for his diet of small animals unless he was near starvation, but at that moment he was. He was also thirsty.

1903 was a dry year, when rats in prolific numbers left their haunts in search of water. In fact, the year was so dry they said even that a rat with an itch could start a fire with the shine of his eyes. Rubbing two blades of grass sparked a conflagration.

The rats searched for water. Chowt hungered for the fresh coolness of spring water. So he followed the rats through Dume

Canyon, along the split-rock cliffs beside the Pacific Ocean. There was plenty of ocean to drink, but the rats knew as well as Chowt to scamper down the ocean edge, to other places, darting back and forth. Chowt sat down on a rock and waited for them to make up their minds. The little water wands didn't seem to be in any great hurry.

Chowt was a little man, small even as Indians go, and appeared to be a large bird poised on the rock, with his tiny legs drawn up under him.

The rats angled up a burned slope. Chowt followed. They ignored him. He was too far away to be attacked, but close enough to see the hundreds of gray bits of coarse fur, slipping in and out among the rocks, clinging with long tails and claw feet, always upward on the smooth slope, bypassing the boulders, going around the steep upward crags, speckling the side of the hill. They angled back and forth, but their general direction was to the north, from where even Chowt could smell water.

It took them two days to reach the top of the hill. They drank the meager dew at night, ate the same wild oats Chowt ate, and chewed on the same berry bushes. Chowt's body craved meat, but he waited patiently for them to find water before he would devour the water wands.

Chowt could see higher hills, even a few mountains to the north, but the rats seemed to prefer this particular hill, which climbed abruptly toward the ocean, ending in a sharp, high cliff facing the Pacific. Chowt knew the hill also ended in an abrupt cliff on the north side. The south slope was covered with gray vegetation, burned by wind, salt, and sun. Toward the east, the hills meandered into other, taller hills. But the rats went north, where a five-hundred-foot drop awaited them.

They continued onto a rock jutting out ten feet or so above the northeast canyon floor and disappeared. Others traveled over the top until all the rats had disappeared. None fell into the canyon, therefore Chowt knew they had found their gold.

Chowt waited patiently, in case the rats came out. During the night he heard them scurrying about, eating grass seeds, and then hiding again before the sun lightened the sky.

Chowt waited for the sun to come up, to evaporate any dew that might make the rocks slick. Then he walked casually to the top of the boulder, squatted, leaned over to see a small cave entrance large enough for any midget Indian named Zuma Chowt.

Slowly he swung himself down, with nothing but a half thousand feet of air below him, and clung to the rock with lichen tenacity, hanging by the sweat of his fingers. His feet swung blindly toward the rocky lip below the cave entrance. With a mighty swing he heaved himself feetfirst into the cave.

He crawled backward, listening, hearing the gush of liquid echoing in the silent cave. Every few feet he swept his short arms above him, judging the ever-increasing height of the cave ceiling. Then he stood erect in the damp stillness.

Dark encircled him completely as he felt along the side of the cave until water splashed onto his hand. He smelled the water before he drank, then felt with his feet to find where the spring splashed from the cave wall; he stood under the cold water and murmured pleasures. On hands and knees he followed the stream to its outlet in the rocks.

The next few weeks Chowt spent trying to get out of the cave. He made the inside of the mountain into a molehill in his desperate struggle for survival. He pounded the walls, listening for the dull, flat sound that said dirt instead of rock, a place to dig for an opening, an escape.

Using his strong, thin fingers, he clawed and dug at the dirt that faced the ocean, because a deep cleft in the rock floor

indicated that at one time the water had emptied into the ocean
through a waterfall which had been shunted aside during some
past earthquake. Somewhere in that rocky cliff there must still
be an opening.

When hunger gnawed at him, he sat quietly, waiting for the
rats to attack. Then he pounced and came out the victorious
diner. But the supply of rats was rapidly becoming exhausted,
and still he had not found an exit.

Then one day Chowt's raw and bleeding hands dug into
dirt and returned filled with nothing but salty ocean air. He
peeked through the hole to see the sun setting on a brilliant
ocean. He ripped his clothing apart, made a rope, and swung
down.

In the months that followed, Chowt decided that the better
part of valor—eluding the white man—would be to make the
cave his home. He stole ropes and spades from nearby villages
and returned to the cave.

He would sit on the top of the hill and contemplate his
home and stare for long hours at the ocean which crashed
against the cliff below. Then one day he shoved a few stones
here and there, placing them carefully at the top of the hill where
the cracked stone layered beneath the thin vegetation. Then he
swung down to the bottom of the cliff and stood in the surf,
looking upward. Carefully he shoved stones here and about.
Though the rocks appeared to be shoved at random, he had a
plan.

When he went topside again, he broke small stones loose
from beside and beneath the larger ones, and suddenly it seemed
that the whole cliff was tumbling into the ocean.

He waited until the dust had subsided, then looked down at
the debris he had created. The top of the hill was now
reasonably flat, and as the stones and boulders had fallen they
had crashed into the smaller ones he'd placed so carefully, thus

changing the course of the stones so they landed in a haphazard V in the ocean.

He sat for a long time in the cliff opening, waiting for the tide to come in, and when it did the water roared into his inlet with a vengeance. He tossed out a long piece of twine with a fishhook on the end.

But along with the man-made fishing hole came an unexpected problem. The tide rushed into the V-shaped inlet and, with nowhere else to go, rose with a roar, splashing water halfway up the cliff. During storms the waves would expend themselves, with a mighty heave, into the cave itself.

Luckily, however, storms were infrequent, and with his stolen spade he dug dirt from inside his new home, moved rocks, chiseled, and finally fashioned a commodious place which, though dark and cool, was periodically washed by ocean storms.

He dug out the other veins of the cave. He stopped fighting the white man long enough to settle peaceably in Dume Canyon.

Once or twice a year he walked to Oxnard to earn or steal oddments of clothing. He was past the time when the pecking between races excited him, and, too, the white man had become bored and embarrassed by the continual harassment of the remnants of Indian bands.

His female Indian acquaintances wanted nothing to do with itinerant Indians. They had jobs as servants, or returned to the reservations.

During the hot California summers he walked throughout the state, wherever he pleased, looking not unlike a tiny Mexican—except for the fold of skin across his eyelids and his thin mouth—dressed in a pair of boy's overalls. In winter he improved his quarters.

Dume Canyon, squatting halfway between Santa Monica and Oxnard, improved with the help of Chowt. He trimmed dead branches for firewood, used the dead brush for bedding,

trapped the wild animals that harassed the ranchers, cleaned the cliffs of dangerous rocks that might fall on him, or unsuspecting cowboys, and developed the water source in the cave. He learned to harness the black gold which dripped and disappeared between the rocks inside his cave—and in the discovery, made quite by accident, he almost buried himself alive.

Few people knew that Chowt lived in a cave in Dume Canyon. After two white men fell off the cliff trying to get to him, they decided he was a monument to the judiciousness of the new laws that said Indians hurt nobody.

A few years after Chowt arrived, the state built a road along the ocean, cutting through the rocks at the foot of his cliff home. The builders never realized Chowt was watching them from behind the dead branches that camouflaged his cave opening.

Civilization closed in on Chowt after that first road was built. It hurt him to see a wagon and team of mules, then eventually a car or two, drive past, filled with people. Though he mellowed and became like a bonsai—tiny, pruned, seeming to live forever as an unseen gray ghost—civilization hurt him. When there had been no one, it had been easier; now he felt an ache, like a missing leg, a missing arm; he longed for human laughter, a human voice.

One day he returned to the cave with a friend, a fellow Indian, but after a year or two the friend couldn't stand the solitude and loneliness, and left. Chowt tried bringing a squaw to live with him, but she couldn't stand him. So he built, and struggled on, until loneliness overwhelmed him again.

One day when Chowt was seventy-five, he raided the home of an Oxnard banker, kidnaped the Indian servant girl, and took her for a wife. The older people in Oxnard remembered him then and laughed at the romance of such an old codger. Newspaper people searched old files and reprinted the old stories about him. A master's thesis was written about the one remaining Indian in the area, the goat of the hills. One doctor's dissertation was begun, but when the doctor-to-be tried to climb up to Chowt's cave for an interview, he fell off, after which people decided to leave Chowt alone. Indians were no longer being punished for white men's clumsiness.

And much to everyone's surprise, including Chowt's, the Indian girl stayed with him.

By 1944 he was completely forgotten by the younger generation. He was ninety years old, but still active and well. He had learned a few English phrases from his wife and still made a few trips into Oxnard, but most of his time was spent happily with his wife and daughter, whom he taught to survive in the best way he knew how—through his old Indian ways. His fortress was inaccessible, his life was secure, and he saw no reason to change his ways for himself or his little family. His cave was situated on public land, so no person harassed him about it.

Once a scoutmaster shepherding his troop through the area thought he saw a gray ghost of a woman swinging across the cliffs on a rope, but he refused to admit it to his scouts, and instead told them about Tarzan. A motorist swore he heard a mermaid singing off key, but the motorist had liquor on his breath. An intrepid teen-age rock hound told people how he caught his foot in a trap and a dark woman with a hairy body opened the trap and set him free. But the teen-ager gave up rock collecting and did not return for a second look.

A man named Leo Corrillo offered to finance a public park out of the area, but nobody wanted useless rocks and a cruel surf.

Also in 1944, Chowt's daughter turned fifteen. Her brown skin blackened from the sun, she was a thin shadow climbing over rocks and through bushes, with wild, uncombed black hair and a bloodcurdling scream that practiced peculiar English to the Pacific Ocean. She would swing on a wet seaweed rope firmly anchored inside the cave, or use one Chowt had stolen at Oxnard. Any person seeing her thus move over the face of the rocky cliffs would have sworn he had seen a mountain goat skipping nimbly. And with good reason. She wore garments of fur or skins, having made them according to Chowt's instructions. She balanced herself with the agility of a mountain goat, having learned that from her father too. He taught her how to squat high up in the rocks in the sun, like a gray wildcat, to watch the ocean for food. He taught her everything he knew, and her mother taught her pidgin English.

——

The Indian girl squatted on a rock far up on the cliff to watch what appeared to her to be a log drifting in to shore. She spread her leather skirt about her legs, dug her toes against the rock, and pondered what she could do with that log.

It wasn't the same kind of log one chopped down green or picked up from a dead tree. Driftwood was hard and light.

"I want that log." In her mind she devised various uses for it. She could cut it in half and make two stools. She could burn out the center and make a dugout canoe. She could split it, burn it, make fence posts, a seat, or even a ladder out of it. No, it wasn't a scrubby pine or a limber sapling. It would be pretty, too. She could even float on it out into the ocean and catch fish.

She swung down the cliff on her rope, ran across the rutted road to the beach, and dived into the breakers, her leather skirt clinging to her body like a second skin. As she swam closer she saw a person clinging to the driftwood and as she came up to him he smiled wanly, thinking help was arriving. The girl slapped him across the side of the head, sending him tumbling into the breakers. With one hand grasping the log, she swiftly outdistanced the weary man.

He pleaded, but she was already nearing the beach. Salt water filled his mouth. He sputtered. He turned on his back to float, letting the surf carry him toward the beach, until finally he lay like a half-drowned rat amid the litter of rusty cans, half-buried old fire holes, broken bottles, soggy paper cartons. All with a stench to match.

"Fuckin' bastard!" He lay there shivering, the sand filtering over him in the strong wind, as he waited for his breath to return. He looked about for a place to hide in case the military was searching for him. Down the coastline, shrouded in September heat, he could see the outlines of a military post. He judged the distance to be about five or ten miles. "Goddamn! I didn't desert just to be shot for a deserter!"

The entire beach was as silent as the day Chowt had first stepped upon it. Seagulls perched or stood at the water's edge, backing away when the surf nibbled at their feet. Then they followed the water as it went out again, leaving bits of smelly sewage. They clustered in groups that flew upward to avoid the incoming water, searching to find fish, because they had already picked the rusty cans clean or eaten the last bit of discarded meat. No sunbathers came to this beach any more, because of the garbage and also because its surf dumped clumps of oil and tar from a sunken tanker a few miles offshore.

Sand whirled and dribbled over the rocks, only to be captured by the water as the surf pounded forward. There was a smell of tar and oil everywhere.

When the man finally staggered to an upright position, the seagulls fled. "I wonder where that damn dame come from," he said aloud, but his words drifted into the wind and smashed on the red-rock canyon walls leaning in layers for miles down the deserted shoreline.

He could see the road clinging to the edge of the ocean. But there was no car in sight. "Gas rationing," he said, glad no civilian was about to intrude on his freedom. The eroded stone peaks stood defiantly against the ocean, with only the ribbon of road hanging between.

He stared at the cliffs. No vegetation except bunches of dead bushes dotting the cliffs. Nothing but broken rock— pocked, burned black by wind and sun, or bleached red. No life. To the south, through the haze, he could see what he thought was Santa Monica.

He crossed the road and stood beneath the canyon cliff, where the wind was less fierce. Breakers followed him obediently to the road, fell back. Huge boulders lay to either side of him.

He saw a car coming so he hid among the coarse rocks. There, warm, resting in a pocket of sun, he moaned, laid his head on a bunch of dry grass, and waited for the car to pass. Then he sighed, leaned more comfortably into the warm after- noon sun, closed his eyes, and went to sleep.

Several jeeps full of military police drove slowly back and forth, and had Private Nelson Winks been awake he would have heard them say, "Probably sharks got him." And, "Don't see how he had the strength to make it. Probably drowned."

The girl hid above in the cave, and when Private Winks awoke, the beach once more seemed vacant and captured in silence. He rummaged in his pockets for food, found nothing but a chewed wad of gum and a wet cigarette package. He laid the package of cigarettes on the rocks to dry and popped the gum into his mouth, chewing lint and gum together. The gum still contained its spearmint flavor.

He climbed up onto one of the boulders. Just as he reached the top he fell back, but not before he had seen a service station down the road. "Coupla miles. And I don't see no MPs." His intention was to walk to the service station, but he changed his mind when he heard a jeep nearing from the north.

"Damn, they ain't gonna find me!" He hid behind a

boulder. "Thousand miles of water in front of me, and rocks behind me. No better than a cornered rat."

But the jeep drove by, and his confidence returned. He said aloud, "I can make it to the service station before dark."

Seagulls once more perched around him. Then he heard a noise above. Thinking it was a seagull, he looked up, preparing to duck, but he saw the figure of a girl dressed from head to foot in skins.

"Rat's ass!" he exclaimed, sheltering his head from the shower of rocks. "I know that's a girl," he muttered, "but she don't look like no broad I ever seen." He moved aside as a large rock bounced where his head had been a moment before. "That's the same priss that tried to bash my head in and stole my log. How the hell did she get way up there? She must be half mountain goat!"

She was brushing rocks off the ledge, and they fell like bullets around Winks. He clasped his hands together over his head. "Damn you, you she-ass. I ain't gonna take that!" He reached for a rock and slung it upward. She plucked a rock out of a crevice and threw it at him. He ducked. The rock missed his head but slammed into his leg, knocking him sideways, so that he hit his head against the cliff and crumpled down, unconscious, on a jagged seat.

She sat on the ledge, dangling her feet over the side, now and then nonchalantly peering down at his prone figure. She was very dark, and her long black hair was plaited into a pigtail that coiled like a snake beside her on the ledge.

She heard a call from above, and the face of a woman appeared out of the cave. Her mother said something in her native tongue to the girl and it was ignored as the girl casually swung her feet back and forth. The woman repeated her demand and the girl said, in English, defiantly, "I won't!" It wasn't the kind of flat, angry "won't" a white girl might have uttered, in that there was no stubbornness to her tone of speech. Rather, her voice was coarse and untrained, oddly singsong, as though she'd learned English that had been tuned in to the wind, moving up and down as though the notes had been blown across the top of a bottle. Actually, that was indeed why she spoke English that way—because it had come to her from across the cave entrance.

"You will!" said the older woman, in a softer English than the girl, for the mother had learned her English from people accustomed to speaking it.

"I won't!" said the girl. "Kill him." She picked up another rock, aimed it down at Winks.

The mother said patiently, "I tell you it is a man. A man like your father. It is a man like a husband. It is not an animal to be slaughtered for food. It is a man. A man!"

"White man?" she asked, and the words were strangely harsh against the cliff.

"White man," said the mother.

"Kill, kill, kill, kill," she singsonged. "Kill, kill, kill, kill."

The mother reverted to her native tongue. *"Ubayi na Chowt, na Chowt."* Then she lowered a rope.

The girl pouted, muttered angrily, but climbed down the rope, barely touching the rocks as she swung in and out, shoving with her toes like a ballet dancer. Then she stood beside Winks, looked down at his limp figure, picked up a rock, and pulled back her arm for a good hard aim.

The woman let loose a blistering string of words, clearly condemning the girl. She kept scolding her, chattering like an angry bird, while the reluctant girl tied the rope about Winks. Then the woman began pulling him up the side of the cliff to the cave above.

The girl made no attempt to move the soldier's limp, unconscious body out of the way of the sharp rocks which ripped into his flesh; his blood marked his ascent up the wall.

Then the girl shoved him into the mouth of the cave, tossed the rope in, and went away to sulk on the ledge hewn out of the wall inside the cave. She watched her mother take long thin leaves from a plant and lay them on Winks's bleeding back, on the open wounds the rocks had cut into his shoulders, and where his head had banged against the cliff. She tied the leaves on with green seaweed strings around his head, waist, and chest. She tied his hands together and his feet; then she too went to the ledge and sat down beside her daughter.

They argued, jabbered, chattered—first in their native tongue, then in sprinkles of Spanish, English, whatever language the woman had picked up in the kitchens of her past. There was even a *"mais oui."* However, English came more easily.

The old woman said, "When I came here there were no soldiers, no roads, nothing but water and rock and Henry's tree. Now we got dirty beach and rocks. Trash on beach."

"Trash on beach," echoed the girl. "Trash on beach."

"I sen' you to Mrs. Eli. She teach you white ways of white man," said the mother, not knowing the woman called Eli had been dead for ten years.

"But Dowdy says stay here where Henry only kill," argued the girl. "Henry" was the name they had deciphered from a cross Chowt had once stolen from a church. The cross now occupied a revered niche next to the drops of oil that fell continually onto a rock where, once lit, they burned steadily like a candle might—a spot where the family did its cooking and odd worshiping.

Winks opened his eyes, rolling them in an arc that took in the whole room with a quick glance. On seeing the two women, he yelled. They answered coolly, in quiet words that, even though spoken in English, had a wild quality, perhaps because they blended with the pounding surf. "Pray to Henry," the old woman was saying.

They watched Winks struggle with his seaweed bonds, screaming at them. They did not stir, even when he wriggled across the stone floor to the cave entrance and looked down at the road below. He moaned, inched himself backward, sliding, dragging a seaweed mat they had placed under him.

For a long time he stared at them, the gloom of the cave broken by a single shaft of light from the cave opening, then he whispered in an agonized voice through his pain. "You ain't niggers. You ain't got them flat noses or wide lips, and they ain't got your kind of hair. I know now. I'm on Guadalcanal, and you're natives, and I'm about to be dumped in a stew pot." He began to whimper. The two women did not move.

"Who are you?" he pleaded. They ignored him but continued their jabbering to each other while he tried to add them up to something. "Let me see. . . . I was near Santa Monica when I dove overboard. I know I wasn't rescued. I couldn't have drifted down to Old Mexico because I never lost sight of that string of mountains. But you can't be Americans, because people like you don't live in the U.S.A."

His head hurt, and he wondered if they had smashed it. His hands were tied. They had even knotted the seaweed between his fingers, spreading them until they felt like crabs. The rough weeds with which the old woman had treated his wounds felt like spikes. He looked toward the little oil flame beside the cross. The slow drip would fall on the rocky niche, burn furiously, then almost go out before another drop ignited it again, and the smoke curled up to disappear mysteriously.

"This is a cave," he argued to himself. "I must be near Santa Monica. I remember. I looked up and something knocked me down. You—dressed in skins. Skins! Indians! You Indians? I'll be damned. Indians!"

The old woman looked steadily at him and nodded as she picked up a flat, hollowed-out rock.

He said, "Well, you ain't friendly Indians. How in the hell did people like you keep from gettin' civilized? Where you been? Don't you know there's a world out there?"

The girl picked up another rock, a long flat one shaped like a fence picket.

He ducked, expecting to be smashed. "Cut me loose?" he asked.

The old woman got up and went over to him, her long black cotton skirt swishing. She reached over him and untied a few of the knots that held his hands and arms.

"She understands, I think," he murmured. He picked some of the leaves from his head, smelled them, muttered, and threw them on the floor. "Wonder what kind of junk they doused me with? They must have beat me up."

He sat up and could see more clearly that the cave was fairly well lighted from the large entrance, beside which was set a cross of wood on which were tied bushes, with their roots sticking out into the cave: a removable camouflaging door.

The room extended backward into darkness, but there appeared to be another source of light where the rocks jutted out to semienclose this particular large room, which was about fifteen feet wide and barely tall enough for a man of Winks's size to stand up. He wished he could.

The floor of the cave was covered intermittently with seaweed mats, tightly woven. Here and there throughout this front area, and in the semidarkness beyond, rocks jutted up two or three feet from the floor; they were hewn flat across the top and crudely made articles were set upon them.

His head began to pain him again. "Damn if that junk didn't have some kind of medicine in it." He felt the side of his face, covered with dried blood. It hurt, so he reached for the leaf he'd thrown away and reinserted it under the seaweed strings.

Here and there on the floor he could see reflections of light playing, as though reflected from water, and he wondered if escape would be possible. As his eyes became more accustomed to the gloom, he saw other things—a crude loom made of tree branches that leaned against a wall near the cliff entrance, bearskins and woven mats hanging neatly from wooden pegs in the rock walls.

The old woman slipped up behind him, grabbed his hands, and looped the seaweed around them so quickly Winks could not protest.

"Damn you to hell. If I wasn't aching in every bone I'd bat you one."

The girl walked away into the depth of the cave. The old woman sat down and silently watched him.

Then Winks became aware of the light sounds of tinkling water falling, bubbling, gurgling, dripping. Yet he saw nothing.

The girl returned, having taken off her wet leather skirt, and was wearing a very short, ragged skirt and a sleeveless cotton shirt. As she moved around he saw she wore no underclothing at all, and there was not a hair on her body. The soles of her feet were white and the palms of her hands were white, in contrast to the deep brown of the rest of her.

I hope they ain't cannibals, he thought. Then, expecting no answer, he said, "How long you lived here?"

The girl said nothing, but the old woman said, in her strange singsong voice that flirted up and down like a flute, "Chowt came here fifty years ago."

"Forty, Mowma," said the girl. Winks could scarcely understand either of them because of the way they trilled and spilled their words like water.

"I'll be damned. What do you want to live here for?" He could smell the salt in the air. Ocean air. "How come your old man picked this place to hole up in?"

The old woman turned to the girl, and they threw his words back and forth, trying to translate them. Then the girl said, in a surly manner, "He followed the rats."

"Rats follow water," explained the old woman.

After having listened to their meager conversation, he was beginning to make out their language. They acted as though their oldest friends were the sun, the wind, the stars. There was no human touch about them. They were people in name only.

"How far to Santa Monica?" he asked. "Why don't you live there? I'd go on relief before I'd live here."

They seemed to tire of him suddenly, because the girl walked away to the place where the little pool of oil burned and returned with what appeared to him to be pieces of tiny tree limbs, which she shared with her mother.

"I'm hungry," he said. He might as well have been one of the rocks protruding from the floor of the cave. "I'm hungry!" he shouted. "Is that a stove? What you got cookin'? I want something to eat." His fear of the woman waned as his pain eased, so he shouted, "You goin' to let me lay here and starve? Gimme one of them sprouts to eat."

The woman bit them off, chewing slowly, ignoring him. "Chowt come and you eat," said the old woman.

Winks thought about her words. "Shout come and you eat?" But he'd been shouting and nothing had happened.

Then the woman went to the kitchen niche again and by the light of the burning oil he could see her pick dishes from between the rocks in the wall. She returned with a tray made of seaweed, on which were a few chipped dishes and some coarse spoons whittled from wood.

She set the tray on one of the protruding floor-rocks near

him. He could identify pepper-tree twigs among the woven seaweed of the tray. She set her table.

"You goin' to untie me?" asked Winks.

She returned to the niche for more dishes, this time of metal. She plucked more dishes from a woven bag hanging from a peg between two rocks on the wall. These dishes had the appearance of tarnished, unpolished silver.

Winks turned his attention again to his wounds, which were completely covered by the long strips of leaves and bark. "Whatever medicine man you got, he's better than what they gave me at the dispensary. I'll bet these leaves would even cure the clap!" He looked closely for a long time at his bandages. Then suddenly he said, "You got a bathroom?"

Surely they understood *that* word. The girl looked at her mother, then sat down at the crude table and bit off a piece of stick. She began to chew.

"I gotta go to the john," he repeated. The girl glared, picked up a smooth round stone from a basket filled with rocks, and thew it at him. It missed only because he ducked.

"I gotta go," he said, wondering how Robinson Crusoe had managed. In all his reading about shipwrecks or people abandoned on desert islands this basic bodily function had never been a problem.

He could feel the salt caking on his body, the dried blood. He grunted, imitating a bodily function, hoping. In answer the girl picked up a handful of stones and slammed them at him.

"You are the throwinest female," he muttered.

"I kill him?" the girl asked her mother.

"No. Mrs. Eli had white husband. You have white husband too, and I have grandbaby."

A Geronimo Story

ONE

Most of the scouts were at the corral catching their horses and saddling up. I saw them there, busy, getting ready to go; and the feeling of excitement hit me in the stomach. I walked faster. The dust in the first corral was so thick I couldn't see clearly. The horses were running in crowded circles while the men tried to rope them. Whenever someone threw a rope, all the horses would bolt away from it, carrying their heads low. I didn't see our horses. Maybe Mariano thought that me and my uncle weren't going and he left our horses in the pasture.

For a while it had looked like my uncle couldn't go this time because of his foot: he tripped over a big rock one night when he was coming back from the toilet and broke some little bones in his foot. The "sparrow bones" he called them, and he wrapped up his foot in a wide piece of buckskin and wore his moccasins instead of cavalry boots. But when Captain Pratt came to the house the night after they got the message about Geronimo, Siteye shook his head.

"Shit," he said, "these Lagunas can't track Geronimo without me."

Captain said, "O.K."

128

Siteye sat there staring out the screen door into the early evening light; then he looked at me. "I think I'll bring my nephew along. To saddle my horse for me."

Captain nodded.

The other corral was full of horses; they were standing quietly because nobody was in there trying to catch them. They saw me coming and backed away from me, snorting and crowding each other into the corner of the corral. I saw Rainbow right away. My uncle's horse. A tall, strong horse that my uncle bought from a Mexican at Cubero; my uncle has to have a big horse to carry him. The horses that we raise at Laguna don't get as powerful as Rainbow; but they eat less. Rainbow always ate twice as much. Like my uncle, Siteye is a big man—tall and really big—not fat though, big like an elk who is fast and strong—big like that. I got the lariat rope ready and stepped inside the corral; the horses crowded themselves into the corners and watched me, probably trying to figure out which one of them I was going to catch. Rainbow was easy to catch; he can't duck his head down as low as the others. He was fat and looked good. I put the bridle on him and led him out the gate, watching, careful to see that one of the others didn't try to sneak out the gate behind us. It was hard to swing the saddle onto his back; Siteye's saddle is a heavy Mexican saddle—I still use it, and even now it seems heavy to me.

The cinch would hardly reach around his belly. "Goddamn it, horse," I told him, "don't swell up your belly for me." I led him around a little to fool him, so he would let the air out, then I tightened the cinch some more. He sighed like horses do when you cinch them up good and they know you've got them. Then, when I was finished, all I had to do was drop the bridle reins, because this horse was specially trained to stand like he was tied up whenever you drop the reins in front of him, and he would never wander away, even to eat. I petted him on the neck before

I went to catch my horse. Rainbow was such a beautiful color too—dark brown with long streaks of white on each of his sides—streaks that ran from behind his ears to the edge of his fat flanks. He looked at me with gentle eyes. That's a funny thing about horses—wild and crazy when they are loose in the corral together, and so tame when they've got a saddle on them.

My horse was a little horse; he wasn't tall or stout—he was like the old-time Indian horses—that's what my father told me. The kind of horse that can run all day long and not get tired or have to eat much. Best of all he was gold-colored—a dark red-gold color with a white mane and tail. The Navajos had asked twenty dollars for him when they were only asking twelve dollars for their other saddle horses. They wanted cash—gold or

silver—no trade. But my mother had a sewing machine—one that some white lady had given her. My mother said it sewed too fast for her, almost ran over her fingers. So we offered them this new sewing machine with silver engraved trimming on it and a wooden case. They took it, and that's how I got my first horse. That day he was hard to catch. He could hide in between the bigger horses and escape my rope. By the time I managed to catch him I could hear Siteye yelling at me from the other corral.

"Andy!" he called, "Andy, where's my horse? We're ready to go."

It was almost noon when we crossed the river below the pueblo and headed southwest. Captain Pratt was up ahead, and Siteye and Sousea were riding beside him. I stayed behind, because I didn't want to get in anyone's way or do anything wrong. We were moving at a steady fast walk. It was late April, and it wasn't too cold or too hot—a good time of year when you can travel all day without any trouble. Siteye stayed up ahead for a long time with Captain, but finally he dropped back to ride with me for a while; maybe he saw that I was riding all by myself. He didn't speak for a long time. We were riding past Crow Mesa when he finally said something.

"We'll stop to eat pretty soon."

"Good," I said, "because I'm hungry." I looked at Siteye. His long, thick hair was beginning to turn white; his thighs weren't as big as they once had been, but he's still strong, I said to myself, he's not old.

"Where are we going?" I asked him again, to make sure.

"Pie Town, north of Datil. Captain says someone there saw Apaches or something."

We rode for a while in silence.

"But I don't think Geronimo is there. He's still at White Mountain."

"Did you tell Captain?"

"I told him, and he agrees with me. Geronimo isn't down there. So we're going down."

"But if you already know that Geronimo isn't there," I said, "why do you go down there to look for him?"

Siteye reached into his saddle pack and pulled out a sack full of gumdrops and licorice. He took two or three pieces of candy and handed me the bag. The paper sack rattled when I reached into it, and my horse shied away from the noise. I lost my balance and would have fallen off, but Siteye saw and he grabbed my left arm to steady me. I dismounted to pick up the bag of candy; only a few pieces had spilled when it fell. I put them in my mouth and held the quivering horse with one hand and rattled the paper bag with the other. After a while he got used to the sound and quit jumping.

"He better quit that," I said to Siteye after we started again. "He can't jump every time you give me a piece of candy."

Siteye shook his head. "Navajo horses. Always shy away from things." He paused. "It will be a beautiful journey for you. The mountains and the rivers. You've never seen them before."

"Maybe next time I come we'll find Geronimo," I said.

"Umm." That's all Siteye said. Just sort of grunted like he didn't agree with me but didn't want to talk about it either.

We stopped below Owl's Rock to eat; Captain had some of the scouts gather wood for a fire, and he pulled a little tin pot out of his big leather saddle bag. He always had tea, Siteye said. No matter where they were or what kind of weather. Siteye handed me a piece of dried deer meat; he motioned with his chin toward Captain.

"See that," he said to me, "I admire him for that. Not like a white man at all; he has plenty of time for some tea."

It was a few years later that I heard how some white people felt about Captain drinking Indian tea and being married to a

Laguna woman. "Squaw man." But back then I wondered what Siteye was talking about.

"Only one time when he couldn't have tea for lunch. When Geronimo or some Apache hit that little white settlement near the Mexican border." Siteye paused and reached for the army-issue canteen by my feet. "That was as close as the Apaches ever got. But by the time we got there the people had been dead at least three days. The Apaches were long gone, as people sometimes say."

It was beautiful to hear Siteye talk; his words were careful and thoughtful, but they followed each other smoothly to tell a good story. He would pause to let you get a feeling for the words; and even silence was alive in his stories.

"Wiped out—all of them. Women and children. Left them laying all over the place like sheep when coyotes are finished with them." He paused for a long time and carefully rewrapped the jerky in the cheesecloth and replaced it in the saddle pouch. Then he rolled himself a cigarette and licked the wheat paper slowly, using his lips and tongue.

"It smelled bad. That was the worst of it—the smell."

"What was it like?" I asked him.

"Worse than a dead dog in August," he said, "an oily smell that stuck to you like skunk odor. They even left a dead man in the well so I had to ride back four miles to Salado Creek to take a bath and wash my clothes." He lit the cigarette he'd just rolled and took a little puff into his mouth. "The Ninth Cavalry was there. They wanted Captain to take us scouts and get going right away."

Siteye offered me the Bull Durham pouch and the wheat papers. I took them and started making a cigarette; he watched me closely.

"Too much tobacco," he said, "no wonder yours look like tamales."

I lit the cigarette and Siteye continued.

"The smell was terrible. I went over to Captain and I said, 'Goddamn it, Captain, I have to take a bath. This smell is on me.' He was riding around with his handkerchief over his mouth and nose so he couldn't talk—he just nodded his head. Maybe he wanted to come with us, but he had to stay behind with the other officers who were watching their men dig graves. One of the officers saw us riding away and he yelled at us, but we just kept going because we don't have to listen to white men." There was a silence like Siteye had stopped to think about it again. "When we got back one of the officers came over to me; he was angry. 'Why did you go?' he yelled at me. I said to him, 'That dirty smell was all over us. It was so bad we knew the coyotes would come down from the hills tonight to carry us away—mistaking us for rotten meat.' The officer was very upset—maybe because I mentioned rotten meat, I don't know. Finally he rode away and joined the other officers. By then the dead were all buried and the smell was already fading away. We started on the trail after the Apaches, and it is a good thing that scouts ride up ahead because they all smelled pretty bad—especially the soldiers who touched the dead. 'Don't get down wind from the army.' That's what we said to each other the rest of the week while we hunted Geronimo."

TWO

We started to ride again. The sun had moved around past us, and in a few more hours it would be dark. Siteye rode up front to talk to the other scouts and smoke. I watched the country we were riding into: the rocky piñon foothills high above the Acoma mesas. The trail was steep now, and the trees and boulders were too close to the trail. If you didn't watch where you were going, the branches would slap your face. I had never been this far south before. This was Acoma land, and nobody from Laguna would come to hunt here unless he was invited.

The sun disappeared behind the great black mesa we were climbing, but below us, in the wide Acoma valley, the sunlight was bright and yellow on the sandrock mesas. We were riding into the shadows, and I could feel night approaching. We camped in the narrow pass that leads into the malpais country north of the Zuni Mountains.

"Hobble the horses, Andy. We're still close enough that they will try to go home tonight," Siteye told me. "All four feet."

I hobbled them, with each foot tied close to the other so that they could walk slowly or hop but couldn't run. The clearing we camped in had plenty of grass but no water. In the morning there would be water when we reached the springs at Moss-Covered Rock. The horses could make it until then. We ate dried meat and flaky-dry sheets of thin corn-batter bread; we all had tea with Captain. Afterward everyone sat near the fire, because winter still lingered on this high mesa where no green leaves or new grass had appeared. Siteye told me to dig a trench for us, and before we lay down, I buried hot coals under the dirt in the bottom of the trench. I rolled up in my blanket and could feel the warmth beneath me. I lay there and watched the stars for a long time. Siteye was singing a spring song to the stars; it was an old song with words about rivers and oceans in the sky. As I was falling asleep I remember the Milky Way—it was an icy snow river across the sky.

THREE

The lava flow stretches for miles north to south; and the distance from east to west is difficult to see. Small pines and piñons live in places where soil has settled on the black rock; in these places there are grasses and shrubs; rabbits and a few deer live there. It is a dark stone ocean with waves and ripples and deep holes. The Navajos believe that the lava is a great pool of blood from a dangerous giant whom the Twin Brothers killed a long time ago. We rode down the edge of the lava on a trail below the sandrock cliffs which rise above the lava; in some places there is barely room for two horses to pass side by side. The black rock holds the warmth of the sun, and the grass and leaves were turning green faster than the plants and bushes of the surrounding country.

When we stopped for lunch we were still traveling along the edge of the lava. I had never walked on it, and there is something about seeing it that makes you want to walk on it—to see how it feels under your feet and to walk in this strange place. I was careful to stay close to the edge, because I know it is easy to lose sight of landmarks and trails. Pretty soon Siteye came. He was walking very slowly and limping with his broken foot. He sat down on a rock beside me.

"Our ancestors have places here," he commented as he looked out over the miles of black rock. "In little caves they left pottery jars full of food and water. These were places to come when somebody was after you." He stood up and started back slowly. "I suppose the water is all gone now," he said, "but the corn might still be good."

When we finally left the lava flow behind us and moved into the foothills of the Zuni Mountains, Siteye looked behind us over the miles of shining black rock. "Yes," he said, "it's a pretty good place. I don't think Geronimo would even travel out there."

Siteye had to ride up front most of the time after we entered the Zuni Mountains. Captain didn't know the trail, and Sousea wasn't too sure of it. Siteye told me later on he wasn't sure either, but he knew how to figure it out. That night we camped in the high mountains, where the pines are thick and tall. I lay down in my blanket and watched the sky fill with heavy clouds;

and later in the night, rain came. It was a light, spring rain that came on the mountain wind. At dawn the rain was gone, and I still felt dry in my blanket. Before we left, Siteye and Captain squatted in the wet mountain dirt, and Siteye drew maps near their feet. He used his forefinger to draw mountains and canyons and trees.

Later on, Siteye told me, "I've only been this way once before. When I was a boy. Younger than you. But in my head, when I close my eyes, I can still see the trees and the boulders and the way the trail goes. Sometimes I don't remember the distance—things are closer or farther than I had remembered them, but the direction is right."

I understood him. Since I was a child my father had taught me, and Siteye had taught me, to remember the way: to remember how the trees look—dead branches or crooked limbs; to look for big rocks and to remember their shape and their color; and if there aren't big rocks, then little ones with pale-green lichens growing on them. To know the trees and rocks all together with the mountains and sky and wildflowers. I closed my eyes and tested my vision of the trail we had traveled so far. I could see the way in my head, and I had a feeling for it too—a feeling for how far the great fallen oak was from Mossy Rock springs.

"Once I couldn't find the trail off Big Bead Mesa. It was getting dark. I knew the place was somewhere nearby; then I saw an old gray snake crawling along a sandy wash. His rattles were yellow brown and chipped off like an old man's toenails." Siteye rearranged his black felt hat and cleared his throat. "I remembered him. He lived in a hole under a twisted tree at the top of the trail. The night was getting chilly, because it was late September. So I figured that he was probably going back to his hole to sleep. I followed him. I was careful not to get too close—that would have offended him, and he might have gotten angry and gone somewhere else just to keep me away from his hole. He took me to the trail." Siteye laughed. "I was just a little kid then, and I was afraid of the dark. I ran all the way down the trail, and I didn't stop until I got to my house."

FOUR

By sundown we reached Pie Town. It didn't look like Geronimo had been there. The corrals were full of cows and sheep; no buildings had been burned. The windmill was turning slowly, catching golden reflections of the sun on the spinning wheel. Siteye rode up front with Sousea and Captain. They were looking for the army that was supposed to meet us here. I didn't see any army horses, but then I didn't see any horses at all. Then a soldier came out of the two-story house; he greeted Captain and they talked. The soldier pointed toward the big arroyo behind the town.

Captain told us that they were keeping all the horses in a big corral in the arroyo because they expected Geronimo any time. We laughed while we rode down the sloping path into the wide arroyo. Siteye handed me Captain's sorrel mare and Rainbow for me to unsaddle and feed. I filled three gunny-sack feed bags with crushed corn that I found in the barn. I watched them eat—tossing their heads up in the air and shaking the bags to reach the corn. They stood still when it was all gone, and I pulled the feed bags off over their ears. I took the feed bags off the other Laguna horses, then I tossed them all a big pile of hay. In the other half of the big corral the Pie Town horses and army mounts had gathered to watch the Laguna horses eat. They watched quietly. It was dark by the time I finished with the horses, and everyone else had already gone up to the big house to eat. The shadows in the arroyo were black and deep. I walked slowly, and I heard a mourning dove calling from the tamarack trees.

They would have good food, I knew that. This place was named for the good pies that one of the women could make. I knocked on the screen door, and inside I could see an old white woman in a red checkered dress; she walked with a limp. She opened the door and pointed toward the kitchen. The scouts were eating in there, except for Captain who was invited to eat with the white people in the dining room. I took a big plate from the end of the table and filled it up with roast meat and beans; on the table there were two plates of hot, fresh bread. There was plenty of coffee, but I didn't see any pies. Siteye finished and pushed his plate aside; he poured himself another cup of coffee.

"Looks like all the white people in this area moved up here from Quemado and Datil. In case Geronimo comes. All crowded together to make their last stand." Siteye laughed at his own joke. "It was some Major Littlecock who sent out the Apache alert. He says he found an Apache campsite near here. He wants us to lead him to Geronimo." Siteye shook his head. "We aren't hunting deer," he said, "we're hunting people. With deer I can say, 'Well, I guess I'll go to Pie Town and hunt deer,' and I can probably find some around here. But with people you must say, 'I want to find these people—I wonder where they might be.'"

Captain came in. He smiled. "We tried to tell him. Both of us."

Siteye nodded his head. "Captain even had me talk to him, and I told him in good English, I said, 'Major, it is so simple. Geronimo isn't even here. He's at White Mountain. They are still hunting meat,' I told him. 'Meat to dry and carry with them this spring.'"

Captain was sitting in the chair beside me. He brought out his tobacco and passed it around the table. We all rolled ourselves a cigarette. For a while nobody said anything; we all sat there smoking and resting our dinner.

Finally Mariano said, "Hey, where are we going to sleep tonight? How about this kitchen?"

"You might eat everything," Siteye answered.

"I think it will be O.K. to sleep in the kitchen," Captain said.

Then Major Littlecock came in. We all stared, and none of us stood up for him; Laguna scouts never did that for anyone. Captain didn't stand up, because he wasn't really in the army either—only some kind of civilian volunteer that they hired because once he had been in their army. Littlecock wasn't young; he was past thirty and his hair was falling out. He was short and pale, and he kept rubbing his fingertips together.

He spoke rapidly. "I will show you the Apache camp in the morning. Then I want you to track them down and send a scout back to lead me to the place. We'll be waiting here on alert." He paused and kept his eyes on the wall above our heads. "I can understand your error concerning Geronimo's location. But we have sophisticated communications—so I couldn't expect you to be aware of Geronimo's movements."

He smiled nervously, then with great effort he examined us. We were wearing our Indian clothes—white cotton pants, calico shirts, and woven Hopi belts. Siteye had his black wide-brim hat, and most of us were wearing moccasins.

"Weren't you boys issued uniforms?" the Major asked.

Siteye answered him. "We wear them in the winter. It's too hot for wool now."

Littlecock looked at Captain. "Our Crow Indian boys preferred their uniforms," he said.

There was silence. It wasn't hostile, but nobody felt like saying anything—I mean, what was there to say? Crow Indian scouts like army uniforms, and Laguna scouts wear them only if it gets cold. Finally Littlecock moved toward the door to leave.

Captain stood up. "I was thinking the men could sleep here

in the kitchen, Major. It would be more comfortable for them."

Littlecock's face was pale; he moved stiffly. "I regret, Captain, that isn't possible. Army regulations on using civilian quarters—the women," he said, "you know what I mean. Of course, Captain, you're welcome to sleep here." Littlecock smiled, he was looking at all of us: "You boys won't mind sleeping with the horses, will you?"

Siteye looked intently at the Major's face and spoke to him in Laguna. "You are the one who has a desire for horses at night, Major, you sleep with them."

We all started laughing.

Littlecock looked confused. "What did he say, Captain Pratt? Could you translate that for me, please?" His face was red and he looked angry.

Captain was calm. "I'm sorry, Major, but I don't speak the Laguna language very well. I didn't catch the meaning of what Siteye said."

Littlecock knew he was lying. He faced Captain squarely and spoke in a cold voice. "It is very useful to speak the Indian languages fluently, Mr. Pratt. I have mastered Crow and Arapaho, and I was fluent in Sioux dialects before I was transferred here." He looked at Siteye, then he left the room.

We got up from the table. Siteye belched loudly and rearranged his hat. Mariano and George reached into the woodbox by the stove and made little toothpicks for themselves out of the kindling chips.

We walked down the arroyo, joking and laughing about sleeping out with the horses instead of inside where the white soldiers were sleeping.

"Remind me not to come back to this place," Mariano said.

"I only came because they pay me," George said, "and next time they won't even be able to pay me to come here."

Siteye cleared his throat. "I am only sorry that the Apaches aren't around here," he said. "I can't think of a better place to wipe out. If we see them tomorrow we'll tell them to come here first."

We were all laughing, and we felt good saying things like this. "Anybody can act violently—there is nothing to it; but not every person is able to destroy his enemy with words." That's what Siteye always told me, and I respect him.

We built a big fire to sit around. Captain came down later and put his little teapot in the hot coals; for a white man he could talk the Laguna language pretty good, and he liked to listen to the jokes and stories, though he never talked much himself. And Siteye told me once that Captain didn't like to brew his Indian tea around white people. "They don't approve of him being married to an Indian woman and they don't approve of Indian tea, either." Captain drank his tea slowly and kept his eyes on the flames of the fire. A long time after he had finished the tea he stood up slowly. "Sleep good," he said to us, and he rolled up in his big gray Navajo blanket. Siteye rolled himself another cigarette, while I covered the hot coals with sand and laid our blankets on top.

Before I went to sleep I said to Siteye, "You've been hunting Geronimo for a long time, haven't you? And he always gets away."

"Yes," Siteye said, staring up at the stars, "but I always like to think that it's us who get away."

At dawn the next day Major Littlecock took us to his Apache campsite. It was about four miles due west of Pie Town, in the pine forest. The cavalry approached the area with their rifles cocked, and the Major was holding his revolver. We followed them closely.

"Here it is." Littlecock pointed to a corral woven with cedar branches. There was a small hearth with stones around it; that was all.

Siteye and Sousea dismounted and walked around the place without stopping to examine the hearth and without once stopping to kneel down to look at the ground more closely. Siteye finally stopped outside the corral and rolled himself a cigarette; he made it slowly, tapping the wheat paper gently to get just the right distribution of tobacco. I don't think I ever saw him take so long to roll a cigarette. Littlecock had dismounted and was walking back and forth in front of his horse, waiting. Siteye lit the cigarette and took two puffs of it before he walked over to Captain. He shook his head.

"Some Mexican built himself a sheep camp here, Captain, that's all." Siteye looked at the Major to make certain he would hear. "No Geronimo here, like we said."

Pratt nodded his head.

Littlecock mounted; he had lost, and he knew it. "Accept my apology for this inconvenience, Captain Pratt. I simply did not want to take any chances."

He looked at all of us; his face had a troubled, dissatisfied look; maybe he was wishing for the Sioux country up north, where the land and the people were familiar to him.

Siteye felt the same. "If he hadn't of killed them all off, he could still be up there chasing Sioux; he might have been pretty good at it."

It was still early in the day; the forest smelled green and wet. I got off my horse to let him drink in the little stream. The water was splashing and shining in sunlight that fell through the treetops. I knelt on a mossy rock and felt the water. Cold water—a snow stream. I closed my eyes and I drank it. "Precious and rare," I said to myself, "water that I have not tasted, water that I may never taste again."

The rest of the scouts were standing in the shade discussing something. Siteye walked over to me.

"We'll hunt," he said. "Good deer country down here."

By noontime there were six bucks and a fat doe hanging in the trees near the stream. We ate fresh liver for lunch and afterward I helped them bone out the meat into thin strips, and Sousea salted it and strung it on a cotton line; he hung it in the sun and started to dry it. We stayed all afternoon, sleeping and talking. Before the sun went down I helped Sousea put the pounds of salted meat strips into gunny sacks and tie them on the kitchen burros, who hardly had anything left to carry. When we got back to Pie Town it had been dark for a long time.

In the morning the white ladies made us a big meal; we took a long time to eat, and it was almost noon before we started northeast again. We went slowly and stopped early so Sousea could hang the meat out to dry for a few hours each day. When we got back to Flower Mountain I could see Laguna on the hill in the distance.

"Here we are again," I said to Siteye.

We stopped. Siteye turned around slowly and looked behind us at the way we had come: the canyons, the mountains, the rivers we had passed. We sat there for a long time remembering the way, the beauty of our journey. Then Siteye shook his head gently. "You know," he said, "that was a long way to go for deer hunting."

–Simon J. Ortiz

The End of
Old Horse

Old Horse just wouldn't let go. He kept chewing at the rope and snarling every once in a while through his teeth. Gilly and I laughed at him. Old Horse, he didn't know when to quit.

Finally we got tired of watching him getting at the rope, and then we went to tell Tony that his dog was going nuts. Tony was nailing a horse stall together for his truck, and he just said that Old Horse was a dumb dog. Gilly said he sure was a stupid dog, hell. He used to like to say cuss words when he was a kid, just like Tony said them. I did too, but I didn't so much as Gilly, although he was younger than me.

We went on down to the creek to cool off, and we forgot about Old Horse, because we figured he'd quit after a while. Anyway, we didn't expect that anything unusual would happen that day. Nothing ever did in the summer. Once in a while we had the grabbing day on the saints' days, and that was pretty exciting, but nothing else practically. Sometimes my father would come home with a funny story, or a story about something that happened to somebody, but most of them we didn't hear, because when my father got into telling it good, my mother would say something in order to change the subject.

145

That's when the story was about something we weren't supposed to hear. Hell, it was probably nothing and we would learn about it anyway, but that's the way my mother was.

Anyway, Gilly and I didn't know something was going to happen. You never find out about important things until they happen, and then it's usually too late to do anything about them. I used to wonder what was the use for important things to happen when it was too late to do anything about them, like to jump out of the way or to act differently or to not think so much about them. But it never worked out like that, and all my mother would do about those important things was to explain them, so we could understand them, she said.

Gilly and I had a good time down at the creek. We were trying to chase some trout upstream into a little trap we had made sometime before out of rocks and a piece of curved tin. We had figured to trap some trout in there and feed them in order to fatten them. We caught a couple then, but they got out somehow, and we tried again this time, but we didn't have any luck. We had a good time though, like I said, and after a while we figured we'd better go home before my father got home from work on the railroad. Gilly had a time washing some mud off his Levis, and I was telling him to hurry when Tony came down the trail to the creek. He wasn't smiling, and Gilly probably thought he'd kind of say something about the mud on his Levis, although Tony wasn't our relative or anything.

Tony, like I said, wasn't smiling or joking as usual, and he looked at Gilly for a moment. Old Gilly was really scrubbing away at his Levis, and Tony reached down and said it looked pretty good, nobody'd notice. Gilly smiled real gladly then, and I was about to say good-bye and we'll probably see you tomorrow when Tony said that Old Horse got choked to death.

Gilly and I just stood there, silent as hell, and we didn't know what to say because of the way Tony said Old Horse was choked to death and nothing after that. I looked at him, but his face was blank, just like my father joked; his face was like a wooden Indian. And then I looked at Gilly. His eyes were really funny, ready to cry, I knew, but he'd hold it back for a long time and then when he did start to cry you would hardly notice it. He was like that a lot, and it used to bother the hell out of me. But everything was quiet, just the creek making noise, and a couple of birds, and then I said that maybe Tony shouldn't have tied him up. That was the wrong thing to say because the next thing that happened was Tony pushed me hard and I fell on my side into some bushes. That was something, and I was frightened like a little kid. But immediately, or right in the next moment, Tony picked me up and brushed me off. I was still kind of frightened, though, and I didn't say anything. Go on home, Tony said then, and he said he was sorry he pushed me. And then he crossed over the creek and walked west alongside it. Gilly and I started for home. We didn't pass by Tony's house, but every once in a while we'd sort of sneak a look over toward where Old Horse had been tied to the clothesline pole. It was getting dark by then, and we couldn't see anything.

Gilly was pretty silent, and I knew he was either crying or about to. I tried to take a sneak look, but I knew he'd notice and be angry with me, so I didn't. But all of a sudden he said, "Shit and hellfire," and spit, and then he started to sob. I didn't know what to say except maybe cuss Tony out for being so stupid. Old Horse didn't need to be tied up; he could have come down to the creek with us, or we could have taken him toward Horse Spring. That was easy. Hell, Tony should have just asked us instead of tying his dog up just like that.

I was pretty mad, too, and maybe about to cry at the same time, so I said to Gilly, "Let's race," and started to run. But he didn't run with me, and I stopped and looked him over and said, "Come on, let's race," but he still wouldn't. He just kept sobbing and hiccupping, and then I said, "The hell with you," and started to really run. I ran hard until my lungs started hurting more than the other hurt. And then I stopped and went off to the side of the road and got sick.

After some moments, Gilly came along. He had quit crying. I was O.K. then, too, and I told him I was sorry I had said the hell with him and I didn't mean it. He didn't say anything, but I knew that he believed me.

When we got home it was already dark, and my mother was more or less angry with us. She told us to wash up and come eat supper. My father looked us over, and he was about to say something to Gilly about his Levis, but he didn't. Usually he didn't, and he wouldn't tell my mother about it, either. He told us about the rabbit hunt that the field chief was having in a couple of weeks. Gilly was all excited about it, and we were all talking about it for a while. And then my father asked about Tony and what was he doing these days. I didn't say anything. Gilly said, "Tony choked Old Horse to death, hellfire," and my mother warned him about that kind of language again. I didn't want to talk about it yet, and my father didn't say anything about it either. I guess he figured, too, that what Gilly said seemed to be the end of everything that happened that day.

–*Leslie Silko*

Bravura

Bravura was a poet. He had packed and was ready to leave the university. "I travel light," he commented as I entered his apartment.

"I'm glad you decided to leave the bells and things behind," I said, gesturing at the tambourines and elephant bells that Bravura bought last summer.

I helped him put his suitcases in the car. "What's in this one?" I asked because it was heavy.

"Books."

"What do you need with them—you're supposed to be going out there to live with the people."

Bravura just laughed.

He stretched out and smiled as we pulled away from the duplex. "You're the native—you lead the way." As we were crossing the West Central bridge Bravura sat up and exclaimed, "The mighty Rio Grande!"

"It's dry." I said that because Bravura was waiting for me to say something.

It was hot and the sky was empty blue. The monotony of 66

149

west put him to sleep. The Volkswagen crawled up the Rio Puerco hill—the car is no damn good for this country.

Bravura woke up when I slowed for the Canoncito turn-off. We bounced and rocked across the Navajo reservation land into the Canada grant. The road was getting worse.

"This is exquisite country! There is a timeless beauty to the pink sandrock and the juniper. I want to write about it all."

"Yeah, well there won't be much else for you to do there."

"I know I'll be able to find what I've been looking for out here. A poet doesn't belong in the university—he belongs with the people and the land."

"I still think you should have shaved off your beard. People out here are suspicious of things like that."

Bravura gave me an impatient look. "The Spanish people out here are accustomed to beards—you forget that."

"But you've got a blond beard."

Bravura ignored that remark and was intently surveying the unfamiliar countryside. As we went farther, the junipers and yuccas were gradually replaced by piñons and little barrel cactus. The flattop plateaus came nearer.

"Piedra Lumbre is right below the rim. Can you see it?" I tried to point it out, but Bravura was looking too far east.

The air smelled like piñon sap and it was much cooler. Bravura hung his head out the window, then he said, "Ginsberg would envy me right now," but he didn't finish what he was going to say because we topped a rocky hill and abruptly entered Moquino.

"Are you sure you don't want to take this extra ten dollars?"

Bravura looked surprised. "I've got forty dollars—that will be more than enough."

I left him waving under the grove of cottonwood trees that

grow around the Moquino post office. Bravura was committed to the idea of hitching a ride to Piedra Lumbre with the mail carrier, because it seemed less alien than arriving in a green Volkswagen. I doubted that the car could make it anyway.

Five days later a postcard came. He said that he hated to disturb me but that he needed some money and a roll of window screen. I figured what-the-hell and left early Saturday morning. At Moquino I stopped at Azy Michael's bar for a Coke and I saw Dan Gonzales.

"What are you doing around here? I thought you were at the university." He still reminded me of Pancho Villa—when I was a little kid I used to be scared of him.

"I'm going up to Piedra Lumbre to see a guy who's been staying there."

"You mean that guy Bravura?"

"Yes, do you know him?"

"Sure, I'm renting him a house." Dan laughed, and I understood why Bravura had written for money. Dan's relatives referred to him as the stingy old Mexican, and it was true that he was rich and never loaned money to his relatives. He had cattle on the Canada grant, but they claimed that he didn't make money off cows; he made it off people.

I asked Dan if any arroyos were washed out, then I left Azy's place wondering how much rent Bravura was paying. It was almost noon, and big, purple rain clouds were gathering in the west. Fine dust poured through the closed windows of the car. The rain always seemed to fall on the mountains above the rim, rarely below. The road went steadily toward the foothills at the base of the plateau rim; it was full of black lava rock, and each arroyo crossing had great boulders exposed.

An hour later I reach Piedra Lumbre. The village was on the edge of a wide, deep stream bed which came down from the rim. Sometimes the road went dangerously near the edge, but there were some old, thin cows grazing along the bottom, and I was confident that I could get out if something happened.

I was looking for someone who could show me Bravura's place when Bravura came hurrying to meet me.

"I thought you might be coming today." He got into the car and pointed toward the church. "My place is over that way."

It was very small, but the roof didn't seem to leak because the whitewashed walls showed no signs of water stains. Bravura had his sleeping bag stretched out on a creaking iron bedframe and springs.

"I would offer you something cold to drink but I don't have a refrigerator. How about some water?" He pointed to a bucket in the corner.

"No thanks, I stopped in Moquino and got a Coke. I saw Dan Gonzales there."

Bravura smiled almost reverently. "He's fascinating. He knows so much about the history of this area. His handlebar mustache makes him look like something from another century."

"Yeah, he's notorious in this area."

"Really? What for? He's so warm and friendly—easygoing. The day I got here he introduced himself and offered to rent me this house."

"How much is he charging you?"

Bravura gazed out the door at the massive back walls of the church, then he smiled. "It really isn't much when you consider the beauty of being able to escape the city and the university and return to the simple life. God, it's beautiful to have quiet, clean air. But it's the people—these simple warm-hearted souls who live here—that make me want to write about Life."

That answered my question. The old Jew Mexican was really taking Bravura. It made me mad, not because of Bravura but because Dan was always doing something like that. During a dry winter he charged two dollars for a bale of hay; on the reservation he managed to trade an old milk cow for a colt and two calves.

"I'll buy you a Coke at the store, Bravura."

As we were walking by the church, a bunch of kids about eight or nine years old started yelling at us. Bravura turned red and walked faster.

"What's wrong?" I asked. "What are they saying?"

"The little bastards." Bravura was talking through his teeth. The kids were laughing and yelling "goat whiskers" at him in Spanish.

"Don't let them bother you. Kids always act that way." As I said that I almost felt sorry for Bravura.

Menardo's store was jammed with merchandise; even the little cash register was crowded by boxes of razor blades and metal racks with bags of candy dangling. You could hardly see Menardo. I got two cans of Coke out of the refrigerator case and set them on the counter.

"Forty cents, please."

I wasn't surprised at the price because Menardo kept them refrigerated, but Bravura got mad.

"You mercenary, how do you expect these people to eat when you charge so much?"

Menardo looked offended and wiped his hands on his apron. "I give them all credit—it's them who owe me something."

We left with our cans of pop.

Bravura let me sit on the chair while he squatted on the floor sipping his Coke. He was still mad at Menardo.

"Who's got the goats?" There was a warm current of air moving through the room.

"Everyone here keeps goats, it's part of their way of life."

I could tell that Bravura enjoyed smelling the goats.

I got the roll of window screen out of the car, and we fixed the window. The flies were confused and made clusters on the new screen.

"Well, I've got to get going—it will be dark by the time I get back. Besides, I don't want to keep you from your writing."

Bravura laughed. "You sure are anxious to get back to the bright lights, aren't you."

That was another thing he liked to marvel at: how the people who are born in this country appreciate it the least, how it takes someone from the outside to really appreciate it.

"I've got a paper due tomorrow."

"Well thanks for bringing the window screen. I'll pay you back the twenty dollars as soon as my folks send a check."

"Let me know how your writing goes."

"I will. I haven't gotten around to anything yet, but I've been busy getting settled."

Bravura stood at the door and waved at me until I went around the church, and then I couldn't see him any more.

– Larry Littlebird
and the members of Circle Film

Saves a Leader

Once upon a time, there lived an old woman.
    She was called Grandmother.
She had no children of her own,
    but among the children of the village,
    she had many friends.
She was their friend because
    she told them stories,
    stories of the old ways, and because
    she made good cookies.

The men were going hunting. It was a busy day.
The women were busy
    preparing food for the hunters.
Even the children were busy.
    The boys tended their fathers' horses.
    They chopped wood for the women.
    The girls carried water and gathered the wood.
All the people were working.

All the people . . . except Lazy Coyote.
He slept by the river.

155

By midday the hunters were gone. . . .
     And still he slept.

Before the dust had settled from the hunters' leaving,
     the children had gathered around
     Grandmother's home.

"Grandmother, Grandmother," they called.
"Our work is finished. Will you tell us a story?"
"Yes," she answered, "but first where is my grandson,
     Slender Rain?"
"You mean Lazy Coyote?"
"Lazy Coyote? Why do you call him such a name?"
"He never gets up early and he sleeps all day."
"He never shares in the work."
"He's lazy."
"It's not right to speak of your brother in such a way.
     Maybe he doesn't know you need his help.
     Little Pinto, go and awaken your brother."

"Children, I have baked cookies for the hunters,
     and also have made special ones for you."

(*They sit in a circle, as a basket of cookies is passed around. The
cookies are in the shapes of different animals.*)

"I will tell you a story of a hunt.
It happened in this village a long time ago.
Many of your fathers and mothers were little then,
     like you are.
In the season of the falling leaves,
the time when the grasses were tall
     and the animals were fat.

When the deer, the antelope, and buffalo were many,
our men who had proven themselves
      made medicine for a successful hunt.
They made themselves look like the animals
      they wished to hunt.
Some men were dressed in buffalo robes
      and others in deerskins,
      and they masked themselves
      with the scent of the animals
      they wished to bring home.

Among the men there was one
      who was thought of as being lazy.
He was not considered a provider for the village,
      or even for himself.
On this hunt, Little Cedar knew that he would
      have to prove himself.
He prepared himself long and well.

The morning of the hunt, the scouts sent ahead
      spotted a large herd of buffalo close by.
Word was sent to the hunters to come at once.
A large buffalo was singled out by the leader.
He succeeded in wounding the bull.
The bull turned, ramming his horse.
The horse fell, knocking the rider unconscious.
The leader was caught apart from the rest of the hunters.

Little Cedar saw the leader as he fell.
He turned his pony and rushed to help him.
Little Cedar raced in front of the bull.
Riding directly into the buffalo's path,

he sacrificed his only pony to save
his endangered leader.

He gained the respect of all our people by his bravery.
He had prepared well. His power was strong.
He was given a new name.
He was named Saves a Leader.

When we all work together
        the power of our people is strong.
And, when our prayers are for all."

The children were playing by the river,
        some were swimming.
As usual, Lazy Coyote lay on the bank napping.
Little Pinto, being the best swimmer,
        tried to swim across the river and back.
He tired and was caught in the fast water
        on his way back.
The children began to yell.
"Help! Help!"
The children's shouts awakened Lazy Coyote.
Seeing his brother in danger,
        he remembered Saves a Leader.
He ran downstream and plunged into the swift river.
Immediately the current caught him.
Fighting the rushing water,
        he reached Little Pinto.
Struggling to keep him afloat,
        Lazy Coyote paddled powerfully toward the shore.
He had saved Little Pinto.

The children were proud.
Little Pinto was proud also of his brother.
The village was thankful and happy.
They were happy for their children.
They were thankful for their children.

To the children he was no longer known as
    Lazy Coyote.
The people now named him He Too Saves a Leader.
Together, the power of the people was strong.
The people were very happy together.

– Leslie Silko

from
Humaweepi,
the Warrior Priest

The old man didn't really teach him much; mostly they just lived. Occasionally Humaweepi would meet friends his own age who still lived with their families in the pueblo, and they would ask him what he was doing; they seemed disappointed when he told them.

"That's nothing," they would say.

Once this had made Humaweepi sad and his uncle noticed. "Oh," he said when Humaweepi told him, "that shows you how little they know."

They returned to the pueblo for the ceremonials and special days. His uncle stayed in the kiva with the other priests, and Humaweepi usually stayed with clan members because his mother and father had been very old when he was born and now they were gone. Sometimes during these stays, when the pueblo was full of the activity and excitement of the dances or the fiesta when the Christians paraded out of the pueblo church carrying the saint, Humaweepi would wonder why he was living out in the hills with the old man. When he was twelve he thought he had it all figured out: the old man just wanted someone to live with him and help him with the goat and to chop wood and carry water. But it was peaceful in this place, and Humaweepi discovered that after all these years of sitting beside his uncle in the evenings, he knew the songs and chants for all the seasons, and he was beginning to learn the prayers for the trees and plants and animals. "Oh," Humaweepi said to himself, "I have been learning all this time and I didn't even know it."

Once the old man told Humaweepi to prepare for a long trip.

"Overnight?"

The old man nodded.

So Humaweepi got out a white cotton sack and started filling it with jerked venison, piki bread, and dried apples. But the old man shook his head sternly. It was late June then, so Humaweepi didn't bother to bring the blankets; he had learned to sleep on the ground like the old man did.

"Human beings are special," his uncle had told him once, "which means they can do anything. They can sleep on the ground like the doe and fawn."

And so Humaweepi had learned how to find the places in the scrub-oak thickets where the deer had slept, where the dry oak leaves were arranged into nests. This is where he and his uncle slept, even in the autumn when the nights were cold and Humaweepi could hear the leaves snap in the middle of the night and drift to the ground.

Sometimes they carried food from home, but often they went without food or blankets. When Humaweepi asked him what they would eat, the old man had waved his hand at the sky and earth around them. "I am a human being, Humaweepi," he said; "I eat anything." On these trips they had gathered grass roots and washed them in little sandstone basins made by the wind to catch rain water. The roots had a rich, mealy taste. Then they left the desert below and climbed into the mesa country, and the old man had led Humaweepi to green leafy vines hanging from crevasses in the face of the sandstone cliffs. "Wild grapes," he said as he dropped some tiny dark-purple berries into Humaweepi's open palms. And in the high mountains there were wild iris roots and the bulbs from wild tulips which grew among the lacy ferns and green grass beside the mountain streams. They had gone out like this in each season. Summer and fall, and finally, spring and winter. "Winter isn't easy," the old man had said. "All the animals are hungry—not just you."

So this time, when his uncle shook his head at the food, Humaweepi left it behind as he had many times before. His uncle took the special leather pouch off the nail on the wall, and Humaweepi pulled his own buckskin bundle out from under his mattress. Inside he had a few objects of his own. A dried blossom. Fragile and yellow. A smooth pink quartz crystal in the shape of a star. Tiny turquoise beads the color of a summer sky. And a black obsidian arrowhead, shiny and sharp. They each had special meaning to him, and the old man had instructed him to assemble these things with special meaning. "Someday maybe you will derive strength from these things." That's what the old man had said.

They walked west toward the distant blue images of the mountain peaks. The water in the Rio Grande was still cold. Humaweepi was aware of the dampness on his feet: when he got back from his journey he decided he would make sandals for himself because it took hours for his boots to dry out again. His uncle wore old sandals woven from twisted yucca fiber and they dried out almost immediately. The old man didn't approve of boots and shoes—bad for you, he said. In the winter he wore buckskin moccasins and in the warm months, these yucca sandals.

They walked all day, steadily, stopping occasionally when the old man found a flower or herb or stone that he wanted Humaweepi to see. And it seemed to Humaweepi that he had learned the names of everything, and he said so to his uncle.

The old man frowned and poked at a small blue flower with his walking stick. "That's what a priest must know," he said and walked rapidly then, pointing at stones and shrubs. "How old are you?" he demanded.

"Nineteen," Humaweepi answered.

"All your life," he said, "every day, I have been teaching you."

After that they walked along in silence, and Humaweepi began to feel anxious; all of a sudden he knew that something was going to happen on this journey. That night they reached the white sandstone cliffs at the foot of the mountain foothills. At the base of these cliffs were shallow overhangs with sandy floors. They slept in the sand under the rock overhang; in the night Humaweepi woke up to the call of a young owl; the sky was bright with stars and a half-moon. The smell of the night air made him shiver and he buried himself more deeply in the cliff sand.

In the morning they gathered tumbleweed sprouts that were succulent and tender. As they climbed the cliffs there were wild grapevines, and under the fallen leaves around the vine roots, the old man uncovered dried grapes shrunken into tiny sweet raisins. By noon they had reached the first of the mountain streams. There they washed and drank water and rested.

The old man frowned and pointed at Humaweepi's boots. "Take them off," he told Humaweepi; "leave them here until we come back."

So Humaweepi pulled off his cowboy boots and put them under a lichen-covered boulder near a big oak tree where he could find them. Then Humaweepi relaxed, feeling the coolness of air on his bare feet. He watched his uncle, dozing in the sun with his back against a big pine. The old man's hair had been white and long ever since Humaweepi could remember; but the old face was changing, and Humaweepi could see the weariness there—a weariness not from their little journey but from a much longer time in this world. Someday he will die, Humaweepi was thinking. He will be gone and I will be by myself. I will have to do the things he did. I will have to take care of things.

Humaweepi had never seen the lake before. It appeared suddenly as they reached the top of a hill covered with aspen trees. Humaweepi looked at his uncle and was going to ask him about the lake, but the old man was singing and feeding corn pollen from his leather pouch to the mountain winds. Humaweepi stared at the lake and listened to the songs. The songs were snowstorms with sounds as soft and cold as snowflakes; the songs were spring rain and wild ducks returning. Humaweepi could hear this; he could hear his uncle's voice become the night wind—high-pitched and whining in the trees. Time was lost and there was only the space, the depth, the distance of the lake surrounded by the mountain peaks.

When Humaweepi looked up from the lake he noticed that the sun had moved down into the western part of the sky. He looked around to find his uncle. The old man was below him, kneeling on the edge of the lake, touching a big gray boulder and singing softly. Humaweepi made his way down the narrow rocky trail to the edge of the lake. The water was crystal and clear like air; Humaweepi could see the golden rainbow colors of the trout that lived there. Finally the old man motioned for Humaweepi to come to him. He pointed at the gray boulder that lay half in the lake and half on the shore. It was then that Humaweepi saw what it was. The bear. Magic creature of the mountains, powerful ally to men. Humaweepi unrolled his buckskin bundle and picked up the tiny beads—sky-blue turquoise and coral that was dark red. He sang the bear song and stepped into the icy, clear water to lay the beads on bear's head, gray granite rock, resting above the lake, facing west.

"Bear
   resting in the mountains
   sleeping by the lake
Bear
   I come to you, a man,
   to ask you:
Stand beside us in our battles
   walk with us in peace.
Bear
   I ask you for your power
   I am the warrior priest.
   I ask you for your power
   I am the warrior priest."

It wasn't until he had finished singing the song that Humaweepi realized what the words said. He turned his head toward the old man. He smiled at Humaweepi and nodded his head. Humaweepi nodded back.

Humaweepi and his friend were silent for a long time. Finally Humaweepi said, "I'll tell you what my uncle told me, one winter, before he left. We took a trip to the mountain. It was early January, but the sun was warm and down here the snow was gone. We left early in the morning when the sky in the east was dark gray and the brightest star was still shining low in the western sky. I remember he didn't wear his ceremonial moccasins; he wore his old yucca sandals. I asked him about that.

"He said, 'Oh, you know the badger and the squirrel. Same shoes summer and winter,' but I think he was making that up, because when we got to the sandstone cliffs he buried the sandals in the sandy bottom of the cave where we slept and after that he walked on bare feet—up the cliff and along the mountain trail.

"There was snow on the shady side of the trees and big rocks, but the path we followed was in the sun and it was dry. I

could hear melting snow—the icy water trickling down into the
little streams and the little streams flowing into the big stream in
the canyon where yellow bee flowers grow all summer. The sun
felt warm on my body, touching me, but my breath still made
steam in the cold mountain air.

"'Aren't your feet cold?' I asked him.

"He stopped and looked at me for a long time, then shook
his head. 'Look at these old feet,' he said. 'Do you see any corns
or bunions?'

"I shook my head.

"'That's right,' he said, 'my feet are beautiful. No one has
feet like these. Especially you people who wear shoes and boots.'
He walked on ahead before he said anything else. 'You have
seen babies, haven't you?' he asked.

"I nodded, but I was wondering what this had to do with
the old man's feet.

"'Well, then you've noticed their grandmothers and their
mothers, always worried about keeping the feet warm. But have
you watched the babies? Do they care? No!' the old man said
triumphantly, 'they do not care. They play outside on a cold
winter day, no shoes, no jacket, because they aren't cold.' He
hiked on, moving rapidly, excited by his own words; then he
stopped at the stream. 'But human beings are what they are. It's
not long before they are taught to be cold and they cry for their
shoes.'

"The old man started digging around the edge of a stream,
using a crooked, dry branch to poke through the melting snow.
'Here,' he said as he gave me a fat, round root, 'try this.'

"I squatted at the edge of the rushing, swirling water, full of
mountain dirt, churning, swelling, and rolling—rich and brown
and muddy with ice pieces flashing in the sun. I held the root
motionless under the force of the stream water; the ice coldness

of the water felt pure and clear as the ice that clung to the rocks in midstream. When I pulled my hand back it was stiff. I shook it and the root and lifted them high toward the sky.

"The old man laughed, and his mouth was full of the milky fibers of the root. He walked up the hill, away from the sound of the muddy stream surging through the snowbanks. At the top of the hill there was a grove of big aspens; it was colder, and the snow hadn't melted much.

" 'Your feet,' I said to him. 'They'll freeze.'

"The snow was up to my ankles now. He was sitting on a fallen aspen, with his feet stretched out in front of him and his eyes half closed, facing into the sun.

" 'Does the wolf freeze his feet?' the old man asked me.

"I shook my head.

" 'Well then,' he said.

" 'But you aren't a wolf,' I started to say.

"The old man's eyes opened wide and then looked at me narrowly, sharply, squinting and shining. He gave a long, wailing, wolf cry with his head raised toward the winter sky.

"It was all white—pale white—the sky, the aspens bare white, smooth and white as the snow frozen on the ground. The wolf cry echoed off the rocky mountain slopes around us; in the distance I thought I heard a wailing answer."

NOTES BY THE CONTRIBUTORS

–R. C. Gorman (Navajo)

I was born and raised on the Navajo reservation in Chinle, Arizona, sometime during the depression years of the 1930s. On both sides of the family I am a descendant of sandpainters, silversmiths, chanters, weavers, and probably, as rumored, talented witch doctors. Art has always been our way of life. My grandfather on my father's side was an Indian trader, and my grandmother was the first Navajo to translate English hymns into the Navajo language. My father, C. N. Gorman, is a well-known painter now teaching at the university in Davis, California. My father was one of the original "Gorman boys" who were the first to bring a car into Chinle and, as I have often been told, the first to bring booze into that area. They were all cowboys. Most of the Gormans, including me, were sent to mission schools.

After graduating from high school in Ganado, Arizona, I attended the Guam Territorial College, Marianas Islands; Northern Arizona University, Flagstaff; Mexico City College; and San Francisco State College. All briefly. I served four years in the navy and once had a studio in San Francisco. I am now living in Taos, New Mexico, where I maintain a studio and own the Navajo Gallery.

Basically, I am a painter. Ninety-two rejection slips from *Playboy* magazine made me decide that I had best write for fun and paint for a living.

–Joseph Little (Mescalero Apache)

If I have little to say, it is only because I have lived for but a short time. I was born of mixed blood on the Mescalero Apache reservation in New Mexico. I grew up there, close to the mountains. When I turned fourteen I ventured to California to begin my studies for the Franciscan priesthood. A product of missionary zeal. The summers I spent at home, working at jobs that would get me back to the mountains, the woods, the open air. It was always a time of cleansing. Somewhere along the way I lost sight of my goal, or maybe began searching for a new one. At the end of six years I returned home.

I did not return for long. I enrolled in the University of New Mexico, and spent the next two years pursuing a degree in English. While at the university, I was drawn to the campus Indian club. Here the Indian students came together to give vent openly to the problems of trying to live within, at times, irreconcilable value systems. We used to refer to it as "cultural shock." A nice sociological tag. It was during this time that I realized that the Indian's plight stretched beyond the dates in the history books.

After graduating, I entered the Indian Law program at the University of New Mexico, and married. Naïvely, I thought that justice existed apart from the prejudices of the ordinary world. At present, I have taken a short leave from my law studies to work for an all-Indian business organization. In time I will return to my law books.

I have learned much about the Anglo race—its philosophies, its religious values, its laws—and maybe not enough about my own. I have learned to live with these ideologies but not necessarily by them. It saddens me that a race that can produce such noble ideals cannot live by them. I am caught between mixed blood, mixed cultures, mixed hopes. In time I will return to the mountains that nurtured me, and become whole again. I am a man. I am an Indian.

Clifton Perkins (Mescalero Apache) and Sam Soce (Navajo) of Circle Film, directed by Larry Littlebird
Photo: Robert Nugent

−*Larry Littlebird* (Laguna/Santo Domingo Pueblo)

Mr. Littlebird writes: "In view of the fact that 'Saves a Leader' was written by a group, an individual biography of me is impossible. I believe you have enough information about Circle Film to serve as a biographical note. There would be very little we could add."

Mr. Littlebird is meticulous about taking no individual credit for the story by Circle Film which is in this volume. Circle Film is an all-Indian company which has already made one, still-unreleased feature, an adaptation of N. Scott Momaday's *House Made of Dawn*, and a number of documentary shorts on Indian subjects. Mr. Littlebird himself, in addition to being director of the company, is also a painter and graphic artist.

–*Simon J. Ortiz* (Acoma Pueblo)

This occurs to me: a necessarily defining practice, defining oneself. But I don't reject it.

This morning it's snowing. Joy said, "It's snowing." Yes, it is. I walked outside just a while ago and watched. Said a small prayer, took a deep breath, shivered my sleepiness away. Fixed coffee and listened to the cats munching at their dry food.

The way I do it is: pay the utmost attention to as many things as possible, note their detail, and breathe them into you. Don't worry about leaving some items out; you are only humble and among many parts and forms. And then I tell about them.

It is probably snowing at Acoma, too, my mother's home. I grew there for the first twenty years of my living. That's where the language comes from. On a snow morning someone would say, "It must have snowed last night." "Yes, it must have snowed." Sometimes, on mornings like that, my father and my brothers would track rabbits and dig them out of damp soil near the river. I tell about those things, using that language.

Language is a way of life. I do not wish to regard language merely as a mechanically functional tool, but as a way of life which is a path, a trail which I follow in order to be aware as much as possible of what is around me and what part I am in that life.

I never decided to become a poet. An old-man relative with a humpback used to come to our home when I was a child, and he would carry me on his back. He told stories. My mother has told me that. That contact must have contributed the language of myself.

The way I try to do it with my poetry, my stories, my verbal telling is: realize the obligation that is important, that the language of a person is a road from inside himself to the outside, and from that outside of himself to inside. It is always a continuing motion, never ending.

I've been a journalist, teacher, for a very short time baker's helper, clerk, soldier in the U.S. Army, college student, laborer, public relations director, and other things. I am mainly writing now, using that language, and giving readings and lectures.

I write for myself, my parents, my wife and children, for my community of kinfolk, that way of life. I must do that to ensure that I have a good journey on my way back home and in order that it will continue that way.

Photo: K. K. Jochim

−*Opal Lee Popkes* (Choctaw)

I am of Choctaw Indian descent. My mother was born in Van
Zandt County, Texas, but her mother came from the Oklahoma
Territory. Before that her parents came from Jackson County,
Mississippi, original home of the Choctaw tribe.

I have Indian relatives in Texas who own oil property. I
asked my mother, who today is eighty-four years old, why we
didn't have any oil property. Her answer: "My relatives were
smart; they married rich Indians. I married an illiterate Irish-
man who gave my oil rights away."

—*Leslie Silko* (Laguna Pueblo)

I grew up at Laguna Pueblo. I am of mixed-breed ancestry, but what I know is Laguna. This place I am from is everything I am as a writer and human being.

　　Born: March 5, 1948, in Albuquerque, New Mexico.
　　Present home: Ketchikan, Alaska.

−*Anna Lee Walters* (Pawnee / Otoe)

My name is "I am living."
My home is all directions and is everlasting.
Instructed and carried to you by the wind,
I have felt the feathers in pale clouds and bowed before the Sun
who watches me from a blanket of faded blue.
In a gentle whirlwind I was shaken,
made to see on earth in many ways,
And when in awe my mouth fell open,
I tasted a fine red clay.
Its flavor has remained after uncounted days.
This gave me cause to drink from a crystal stream
that only I have seen.
So I listened to all its flowing wisdom
and learned from it a Song—
This song the wind and I
have since sung together.
Unknowing, I was encircled by its water and cleansed.
Naked and damp, I was embraced and dried
by the warmth of your presence.
Dressed forever in the scent of dry cedar,

I am purified and free.
And I will not allow you to ignore me.
I have brought to you a gift.
It is all I have but it is yours.
You may reach out and enfold it.
It is only the strength in the caress of a gentle breeze,
But it will carry you to meet the eagle in the sky.
My name is "I am living." I am here.
My name is "I am living." I am here.

I was born in Pawnee, Oklahoma, September 9, 1946. I moved to the Southwest as a teen-ager and find it too much a part of me to ever leave behind. I am married to a Navajo artist, Harry Walters (Na-ton-sa-ka). We have two beautiful sons, Tony, seven, and Daniel, four. (Pawhoes, we call them, since they are part Pawnee and part Navajo.)

I like to paint as well as write. Both allow consistent examination and evaluation of oneself. In all the world, only this is important. But I cannot speak for anyone else, only myself.

—Aaron Scott Yava (Navajo / Pueblo)

Born: May 13, 1946.
Place: Keams Canyon, Arizona.
At present: Living anyplace in Arizona.